Turning Things Around

A Kit Classic
Volume 2

by Valerie Tripp

★ American Girl®

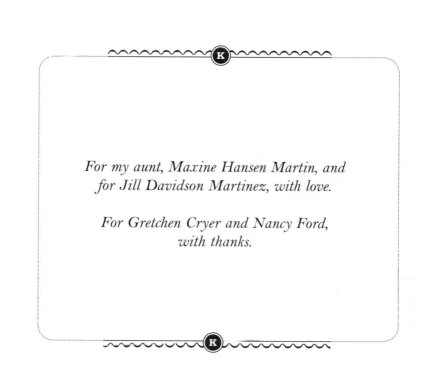

For my aunt, Maxine Hansen Martin, and for Jill Davidson Martinez, with love.

For Gretchen Cryer and Nancy Ford, with thanks.

Beforever

Beforever is about making connections.
It's about exploring the past, finding your
place in the present, and thinking about the
possibilities your future can bring. And it's about
seeing the common thread that ties girls from
all times together. The inspiring characters you
will meet stand up for what they care about
most: Helping others. Protecting the earth.
Overcoming injustice. Through their courageous
stories, discover how staying true to your own
beliefs will help make your world better
today—and tomorrow.

�֎ TABLE *of* CONTENTS ✖

1   Secrets and Surprises 1

2   The Waste-Not, Want-Not Almanac 15

3   Grace 28

4   Penny-Pincher Party 43

5   Stuck 56

6   Just Plain Will 68

7   The Hobo Jungle 81

8   Do Something 95

9   Something Wonderful 109

10   To Do 125

11   Letters with an "S" 136

12   The Perfect Word 147

Inside Kit's World 160

Ⓚ

Secrets and Surprises

❉ CHAPTER 1 ❉

it Kittredge grinned at the headline she
had typed:

Spring Arrivals

Spring, she thought. *Now there is a word with some
bounce to it.*

It was a sunny Saturday morning in April. Kit was
sitting at the desk in her attic room with all the windows wide open to the spring breezes. She and her best
friend, Ruthie, were making a newspaper. What Kit
was *supposed* to be making was her *bed,* but the newspaper was much more fun. Kit loved to write. She loved to
call attention to what was new, or important, or remarkable. So, as often as she could, Kit made a newspaper for everyone in her house to read.

That was quite a few people these days! When
Kit's dad lost his job nine months ago because of the

Depression, her family turned their home into a board-inghouse to earn money. Eleven people were living there now. Kit's newspapers were read by her mother, dad, and older brother Charlie, two nurses named Miss Hart and Miss Finney, a musician named Mr. Peck, a friend of Mother's named Mrs. Howard, and her son, Stirling, who was Kit's age. At breakfast this morning, Kit had interviewed Mr. and Mrs. Bell, an elderly couple who had just moved in. Now she was writing an article about them to help everyone else get to know them.

'Let's all wellcome Mr. and Mrs. Bell,' Kit typed. She stopped. "Hey, Ruthie," she asked, "does *welcome* have one l or two?"

Ruthie started to answer. But suddenly, a gust of wind blew in through the window, swooped up all the papers on Kit's desk, and sent them flying around the room like gigantic, clumsy butterflies. Ruthie and Kit both yelped. They sprang up to chase the papers and heard someone laughing.

It was Stirling. "Close the windows!" he said.

"Too late for that," said Kit, laughing with him.

By now the papers had fluttered to the floor. Kit and Ruthie and Stirling knelt down to collect them.

Stirling held up a page that had been cut from a magazine. "What's this?" he asked.

"Nothing!" said Kit, snatching it away.

"Nothing?" asked Stirling, in his voice that was surprisingly low for someone so little and skinny.

"Well," said Kit, "it's . . . a secret."

"Oh," said Stirling and Ruthie together.

Kit thought quickly. Her friends were good at keeping secrets—this she knew for sure. They were trustworthy, and they'd never laugh at her. She decided to let them in on her secret. "Promise you won't tell," she said.

"I promise," said Ruthie, crossing her heart.

"Me, too," said Stirling.

Kit stood next to them so that they could all look at the magazine page together. "It's a picture of a birthday party for a movie star's child," she said. "See? Some of the kids are riding horses, and some are playing with bows and arrows, and they're all dressed like characters from *Robin Hood*."

"Your favorite book," said Ruthie. "Oh, I *love* this picture!"

"Look in the trees," Kit said enthusiastically. "There

are ropes so the kids can swing from tree to tree like Robin and his men. And there are tree houses on different branches. There's even one at the top of the tree, like the tower of a castle. Some of the kids are eating birthday cake up there."

"Wow," said Stirling quietly. He looked at Kit. His gray eyes were serious. "I think I know why this is a secret," he said. "Because—"

"Because my birthday is coming up in May and I don't want my parents to know that I'd love to have a party like this one!" Kit burst out. "It would only make them feel bad. I know they hate always having to say that we don't have enough money."

Ruthie looked sorry, and Stirling nodded. Kit was sure they understood. They both knew that the Kittredges were just scraping by. If Mr. Kittredge's Aunt Millie had not sent them money, the Kittredges would have been evicted from their house right after Christmas because they couldn't pay the bank what they owed for the mortgage.

Kit took one last longing look at the picture, folded it carefully, and put it away in her desk drawer. "Don't forget you promised not to tell anyone my secret," she said. "Especially not my mother. She's so busy now that she has to cook and clean for eleven people." Kit sighed. "I know I can't have a party like the one in the picture. I shouldn't *really* want any party at all. But I can't help it. I do."

"I think," Stirling said slowly, "that it's okay to want something, even if it seems impossible. Isn't that the same as hoping?"

"That's right," said Ruthie. "And hope is always good. If we just give up on everything, how will anything ever get better?"

"Hope is always good," Kit repeated. She grinned and tilted her head toward the drawer where the picture of the party was hidden. "Even," she said, "if it has to be secret."

❈

Ruthie went home, and Kit put Stirling to work drawing a mitt, bat, cap, and ball to go with an article she'd written for her newspaper about the Cincinnati Reds, the baseball team she and Stirling liked best. While he drew, Kit went to work herself. She took the sheets off her bed. She was careful not to tear them.

They were worn so thin that she could almost see through the middles! But there was no money to buy new sheets, and what good sheets there were had to be saved for the boarders' beds.

"See you later," she said to Stirling as she carried the sheets downstairs.

"Okay," said Stirling, busy drawing.

Every Saturday, it was Kit's job to change the sheets on all the beds. She gathered up the used sheets, washed, dried, and ironed them, then remade the beds with clean sheets. Miss Hart and Miss Finney always left their sheets in a neatly folded bundle next to the laundry tubs, and Mrs. Howard was so persnickety that she insisted on doing all of her laundry herself. Even so, by the time Kit had gathered the rest of the sheets and pillowcases this morning, the pile was so big that she could hardly see over the top of it. She couldn't help feeling exasperated when, as she headed to the laundry tubs in the basement, the doorbell rang.

"I'll get it!" she called. Kit waddled to the door and fumbled with the knob. The sheets began to fall, so she hooked her foot around the door to swing it open. When she saw who was standing outside, Kit dropped the pile of sheets and flung her arms open wide. "Aunt Millie!" she cried as she plunged into a hug. "What a great surprise!"

"Margaret Mildred Kittredge," said Aunt Millie, using Kit's whole name. "Let me look at you." She stepped back and eyed Kit from head to toe. "Heavenly day!" she exclaimed. "You've sprung up like a weed! You must be two feet taller than you were when I saw you last July! And still the prettiest child there ever was! It's worth the trip from Kentucky just to see you."

"I'm glad to see you, too," said Kit, practically dancing with excitement as she led Aunt Millie inside. "I didn't know you were coming."

"No one did," said Aunt Millie. "I just took it into my head to come, and here I am, blown in on the breeze like a bug. Now where are your dad and mother? And where's your handsome brother?"

"Charlie's at work, but he'll be home soon," said Kit. "Mother and Dad are cleaning out the garage. We're so crowded in the house now with all the boarders, we need room out there for storage."

As Kit spoke, Aunt Millie put her suitcase and basket in the corner. She took off her hat and coat, put her gloves in her purse, and hung her things neatly on a hook in the hall. She turned and saw the pile of sheets Kit had dropped. "Changing sheets today, are we?" she observed. "Odd to do it on Saturday, with everyone underfoot. Still, it's a good drying day today." She scooped up half the pile. "We'd better begin."

"But Aunt Millie," said Kit as she picked up the rest of the sheets. "Don't you want to say hello to Mother and Dad first?"

"Time enough for that after we get the laundry started," said Aunt Millie. "Work before pleasure. Come along, Margaret Mildred. If we dillydally, we'll waste the best sunshine."

Kit grinned. *That's Aunt Millie for you*, she thought. *Never wastes a thing, not even sunshine.*

Aunt Millie was not really Kit's aunt, or Dad's either. Mother said that calling her "Aunt" when she was no relation was a very countrified thing to do, and that they should call her "Miss Mildred" because it showed more respect. But Aunt Millie pooh-poohed putting on such airs. "Call me anything, except late for dinner," she'd say. And so "Aunt Millie" she remained. Besides, she and her husband, Birch, were the only family Dad had ever known. They had adopted Dad after his parents died when he was a boy. Uncle Birch worked in the coal mine in Mountain Hollow, Kentucky, until he died. Kit's family visited Aunt Millie there every Fourth of July. But Aunt Millie never came to Cincinnati. "Too many people, not enough animals," she always said. So this visit was a big surprise.

"I can't wait till Mother and Dad see you!" said Kit as she put the sheets in sudsy water to soak. "They'll be so glad you've come for a visit."

"Out of the blue," said Aunt Millie. She smoothed her dress, straightened her shoulders, and smiled at Kit. "'Lead on, Macduff!'" she said, pointing up the basement stairs. Kit was used to the way Aunt Millie quoted poetry and Shakespeare right in the middle of a normal conversation. Aunt Millie had been the schoolteacher in Mountain Hollow ever since Uncle Birch died, and she couldn't stop herself from teaching wherever she was.

The sunshine was dazzling after the dimness of the basement. Kit squinted and Aunt Millie shaded her eyes as they crossed the yard. "Mother and Dad!" Kit called. "Come see our surprise!"

Mother and Dad came out of the garage blinking from the brightness and from amazement.

"Aunt Millie!" Dad exclaimed, striding forward to hug her. "How wonderful! I'm glad to see you!"

"I'm glad to see you, too!" Aunt Millie said.

"Miss Mildred, we're honored," said Mother. "It's so kind of you to make the trip. You look well."

"Fit as a fiddle," said Aunt Millie. "And—"

"—twice as stringy," she and Dad finished together.

Dad threw back his head and laughed with Aunt Millie at their old joke. Kit beamed. It'd been a long time since she'd heard Dad laugh so heartily. No one could make him laugh the way Aunt Millie could!

"I never thought I'd see the day you'd leave your home and come to the city," Dad said to Aunt Millie. "How's everybody in Mountain Hollow?"

"We've been through hard times before," said Aunt Millie. "We'll make it through this rough patch. But the town's been hit pretty badly by this Depression. Last week, they closed the mine. Just couldn't make any money from it. When they shut the mine, they closed down the school, and of course my house went with my job, so I lost *it*, too."

"Oh, no!" exclaimed Dad, Mother, and Kit.

But Aunt Millie did not sound the least bit sorry for herself. "My friend Myrtle Peabody's been after me for years to live with her," she said. "So I guess that's what I'll do." She smiled at Kit and tousled her hair. "I just thought I'd come and see how you folks are doing for a while first."

"You are very welcome," said Dad. "Stay as long as you like."

"Yes," said Mother. "You'll stay in our room while you're here. Kit can take you there now for a rest. You must be tired from traveling."

"Heavenly day, Margaret!" said Aunt Millie. "I'm not the least bit tired. And you needn't treat *me* like company. I wouldn't dream of taking your room. I can park my bones anyplace. Just put me in a corner somewhere."

"Dear me, no!" said Mother. She smiled, but Kit saw she was worried.

Poor Mother! thought Kit. *She wants to make Aunt Millie comfortable, but we don't have a room to put her in. The house is full of boarders.*

"Aunt Millie can share with me," Kit offered.

"There's plenty of room in my attic, and an extra bed we can set up, too."

"That'll be jim-dandy," said Aunt Millie.

"I guess it'll do," said Mother, "since it's just for a while."

"Come on, Aunt Millie," said Kit, taking her hand. "I'll show you the attic. You can meet Stirling. He's up there now drawing illustrations for our newspaper." She grinned. "After I finish the laundry, I'll write an article about you!"

❄

Stirling and Aunt Millie liked each other right away. Aunt Millie was a Cincinnati Reds fan, too. When she praised Stirling's baseball drawings, he turned bright pink with pride.

After Stirling left, Aunt Millie said to Kit, "That boy's as scrawny as a plucked chicken now. But you mark my words—he'll grow into that voice and those ears and elbows someday. And when he does, he'll be a handsome fellow."

Kit giggled at the impossible thought of pip-squeaky Stirling ever being handsome. But Aunt Millie had a way of seeing the potential in people and bringing out the best in them, too.

At first, when Dad introduced her to all the boarders at dinner, everyone was shy. They didn't know quite what to make of Aunt Millie, with her wispy white hair, her cheeks as red as scrubbed apples, her twangy Kentucky accent, her funny expressions, and her quotes that sprang out unexpectedly.

When Aunt Millie passed Mr. Peck the mashed potatoes, she said, "Here, son. You've got that 'lean and hungry look.'"

Mr. Peck smiled, but he looked bewildered. So did almost everyone else.

"That's a quote from Shakespeare," Kit explained.

"*Julius Caesar,*" said Aunt Millie. She turned to Mr. and Mrs. Bell. "Didn't I read in Kit's newspaper that you've acted in some of Shakespeare's plays?"

"Indeed, we have!" said Mr. Bell.

"Please tell us about it," said Aunt Millie, looking very interested.

Mrs. Bell told a funny story about Mr. Bell tripping over his sword in a play. That reminded Mr. Peck of the time three strings on his bass fiddle popped during a concert. And *that* reminded Miss Finney of a patient who was an opera singer and sang whenever he called for her. Soon everyone was telling funny stories and laughing uproariously—even Mrs. Howard, whose usual laugh was just a nervous giggle. Aunt Millie's contagious hoot was loudest of all.

Kit looked at Aunt Millie and grinned from ear to ear. *When I wrote my headline this morning,* Kit thought, *I never guessed who the very best and most surprising spring arrival of all would be!*

The Waste-Not, Want-Not Almanac

❋ CHAPTER 2 ❋

he next day, Aunt Millie woke Kit early.

"Come with me," she said.

"Now?" Kit asked groggily.

"Yes! Time to greet the 'rosy-fingered dawn,'" Aunt Millie replied.

Kit swung out of bed and dressed as quickly as she could. Aunt Millie was not wearing the Sunday-best clothes she had worn for traveling the day before. Instead, she was wearing no-nonsense work clothes. Her old leather boots and straw hat had seen better days, and her sweater had mismatched buttons and tidy patches on the elbows. Over her faded, but very clean, flowered dress, she wore a starched and ironed all-over apron. She was holding two empty cloth sacks.

"What're we doing?" Kit whispered as she tiptoed behind Aunt Millie.

"Collecting while the dew is fresh," said Aunt Millie. When they were outside, Aunt Millie handed Kit one of the sacks. "We're going to gather dandelion greens for salad," she said.

"Dandelions?" squeaked Kit. "You mean we're going to eat our lawn?"

Aunt Millie picked out a dandelion green and handed it to Kit. "Taste this," she said.

Kit took a nibble. "Hey!" she said. "It's good!"

"And free," said Aunt Millie. "Let's get to work."

It was just like Aunt Millie to see the possibilities in a weed. *No one in the world is better at making something out of nothing,* Kit thought as she picked.

By the time everyone else was up, Aunt Millie and Kit had filled their sacks with dandelion greens and had also weeded most of the lawn while they were at it. Aunt Millie was a great one for being efficient. That very afternoon, Aunt Millie, Kit, Dad, and Charlie took hoes and shovels out of the garage and started to rip up a corner of the lawn to plant vegetables there.

"Wait!" cried Mother. "I like the idea of growing vegetables. But couldn't we put the patch behind the garage, where people wouldn't see it?"

"This is nice, flat land that gets plenty of sunshine," said Aunt Millie positively. "Things'll grow beautifully here. It's too shady behind the garage."

"I guess that makes sense," said Mother.

Kit could tell that Mother was not pleased to have the lawn torn up right next to her azaleas. The plot for the vegetable garden *was* an unsightly mud patch. Kit herself was doubtful that the little seeds Aunt Millie had brought would amount to anything. The seeds were wrapped in twists of newspaper that Aunt Millie had labeled and packed carefully in an old cloth flour sack. As Kit planted the tiny gray seeds, she couldn't believe they'd become big red tomatoes, orange carrots, green beans, or yellow squash. But Aunt Millie was cheerfully confident that time, sun, water, and hard work would bring about the magical transformation.

"How come you're so sure?" Kit asked her.

Aunt Millie considered Kit's question. "I guess teachers and gardeners are just naturally optimistic," she said. "Can't help it. Children and seeds are never disappointing." She stood and brushed the dirt off her knees. "Save the flour sack," she said. "I'll make you a pair of bloomers out of it."

"Bloomers?" laughed Kit. "Oh, Aunt Millie, you're kidding! I couldn't wear underwear made out of a flour sack, for heaven's sake!"

"And why not?" Aunt Millie asked.

"Well," Kit sputtered, "what if someone saw them? I'd be—"

"Waste not, want not, my girl," said Aunt Millie tartly. Then, like the spring sun coming out from behind a cloud, she smiled. "You'll like the bloomers," she said. "You'll be surprised."

❋

Kit soon learned that life with Aunt Millie around was *full* of surprises because Aunt Millie was full of ingenious ideas. She could find a use for *anything*, even things that were old and worn out. To Aunt Millie, nothing was beyond hope.

"There's plenty of good left in these sheets," she said when Kit showed her the ones that were thin in the middle. It was a few nights later. Everyone was gathered around the radio waiting for President Roosevelt, who was going to speak in what he called a "fireside chat." Aunt Millie was a big fan of President

Roosevelt and his wife, Eleanor, and had asked Dad to move Mother's sewing machine into the living room so that she could sew while she listened. She liked to do two things at once.

"Watch this, Margaret Mildred," she said to Kit. As Kit watched, Aunt Millie tore the sheets in half, right down the middle. Then she sewed the outside edges together. "Now the worn parts are on the edges and the good parts are in the middle," she said. "These sheets'll last ten more years."

The next night, Aunt Millie taught Kit how to take the collars and cuffs off Dad's shirts and sew them back on reversed, so that the frayed part was hidden. Kit was pleased to know how to do something so useful. She was glad when Aunt Millie promised, "Tomorrow night I'll teach you how to sew patches on so they don't show." And Kit was proud when, as everyone was saying good night, Aunt Millie announced, "If you've got anything that needs patching, bring it down tomorrow. Margaret Mildred and I'll take care of it for you."

Kit saw that Mother's lips were thin as she tidied up the room. Kit was puzzled. Since Dad lost his job, no one had struggled harder than Mother to save money.

Surely she appreciated all Aunt Millie's frugal know-how! And yet it seemed that Mother felt the same way about the sewing machine in the living room as she'd felt about the vegetable patch in the yard. It was just too visible.

But Kit thought it was great fun to have Aunt Millie and the sewing machine right in the thick of things. The living room felt cheery and cozy in the evenings with the sewing machine clicking away while the boarders chatted or listened to the radio. Kit liked learning all of Aunt Millie's skillful tricks, like how to use material from inside a pocket to lengthen pants, how to embroider yarn flowers over tears, holes, and stains, and how to darn socks so that they were as good as new. Aunt Millie was a good teacher. She was brisk and precise, but patient.

"I love the way Aunt Millie takes things that are ugly and used up and changes them into things that are beautiful and useful," Kit said to Ruthie and Stirling as they walked home from school one day.

"Just like Cinderella's fairy godmother," said Ruthie, who liked fairy tales. "You know, how she turned Cinderella's rags into a ball gown."

"Aunt Millie uses hard work instead of a wand," said Kit. "But it does seem like she can do magic."

"Maybe you should show her the picture of the Robin Hood party," said Ruthie. "Maybe she could figure out a way to do that."

"I don't think so," sighed Kit. "But she sure has lots of great ideas." Suddenly Kit had a great idea of her own. "You know what we can do?" she said excitedly. "We can write down Aunt Millie's ideas. We'll make a book! Ruthie, you and I can write it, and Stirling can draw the pictures."

"What'll we call it?" asked Ruthie.

"Aunt Millie's Waste-Not, Want-Not Almanac," Kit said with a grin. "What else? The thing Aunt Millie hates most is waste, and it would be a terrible waste if we forgot all she's taught us after she leaves. Writing her ideas down will be a way of saving them. We won't tell Aunt Millie about our book. Then right before she goes home, we'll show her. It'll be a way to thank her."

"Is she leaving soon?" asked Stirling.

"I hope not!" said Kit. "Come on, let's run home and get started before I have to do my chores!"

Kit didn't have a blank book, so she took one of

Charlie's old composition books, turned it upside down, and wrote on the unused back sides of the pages. She divided *Aunt Millie's Waste-Not, Want-Not Almanac* into four sections: "Growing," "Sewing," "Cooking," and "Miscellaneous Savings." In the "Growing" section, Stirling drew a sketch of the vegetable patch. Ruthie labeled the rows, and Kit wrote Aunt Millie's advice about planting, watering, and weeding in the margins. In the "Sewing" section, Stirling drew diagrams to show how to turn sheets sides-to-middle and how to reverse cuffs. Kit wrote out the directions in easy-to-follow steps.

Almost every day there was something new to add to the *Almanac*. Aunt Millie taught the children how to trace a shoe on a piece of cardboard, cut it out, and put the cardboard in the shoe to cover up a hole in the bottom. She showed them how to take slivers of soap, melt them together, and mold them into new bars of soap. She also taught the children to save string, basting thread, and buttons, and to be on the lookout for glass bottles to return for the deposit.

One day, when Kit and Stirling came home from school, they saw a horse-drawn wagon parked in front of the house. It belonged to the ragman, who paid by the pound for cloth rags. Kit had always wanted to get to know the ragman's horse, but Mother never asked the ragman to stop. She said the horse was unsanitary. Aunt Millie, however, was petting the horse and feeding it apple cores. Kit and Stirling were tickled when Aunt Millie let them feed the horse, too.

"'My kingdom for a horse,'" said Aunt Millie, quoting Shakespeare as she petted the horse's nose. She smiled at the ragman. "If I'd known you were coming, I'd have gathered up some rags to sell you. We have some dandies."

The ragman was very pleased by Aunt Millie's kindness to his horse. "I'll tell you what," he said. "I wasn't planning to come back this way next week, but for you, I will."

Kit and Stirling exchanged a glance. Here was a typical Aunt Millie idea to put in their *Almanac*: save apple cores, charm the ragman, and get good money for your rags!

Saturday rolled around, and Kit was delighted when Aunt Millie announced that she and Kit would do the grocery shopping. They set forth after Kit had washed and ironed all the sheets and remade all the beds. Aunt Millie had her hat firmly fixed on her head and her shopping list, written on the back of an old envelope, firmly held in her hand. Kit skipped along next to Aunt Millie, eager and alert. She was sure to hear more good ideas for the *Almanac* on this shopping trip. Kit had noticed before that when she was writing about something, she had to be especially observant. Writers had to pay attention. Everything *mattered*.

Kit's heart sank a little when she saw that they were headed to the butcher shop. The butcher was well known to be a stingy grouch.

"What would you like today?" he asked Kit and Aunt Millie.

Aunt Millie spoke with more of a twang than usual. "I'd like," she said, "to know what an old Kentucky hilljack like you is doing in Cincinnati."

Kit gasped. She was sure the butcher would be angry. It was not complimentary to call someone a "hilljack." But Aunt Millie's question seemed to have worked another one of her magical transformations.

Smiling, the butcher asked, "How'd you know I'm from Kentucky?"

"Because your accent's the same as mine," said Aunt Millie.

The butcher laughed. For a long while, he and Aunt Millie chatted and swapped jokes as if they were old friends.

"Now," Aunt Millie said at last, "if you've got a soup bone and some meat scraps you could let me have for a nickel, I'll make some of my famous soup." She pointed to Kit. "And Margaret Mildred here will bring you a portion. How's that?"

"It's a deal," said the butcher cheerfully.

As they left the butcher shop, Kit hefted the heavy parcel of meat. "Gosh, Aunt Millie," she said. "All this for a nickel?"

"A nickel and some friendliness," Aunt Millie said. "Works every time." She caught Kit's arm. "Slow down there, child. What's your hurry?"

"Well," said Kit, "you and the butcher talked so long, I'm afraid the grocery store will be closing when we get there."

Aunt Millie winked. "I hope so," she said.

Kit was confused until Aunt Millie explained, "Tomorrow's Sunday and the store'll be closed. So, just before closing time today, the grocer will lower the prices on things that'll go bad by Monday."

"Ah! I see!" said Kit.

Of course, Aunt Millie was right. The grocer *was* lowering the prices. Aunt Millie and Kit were able to get wonderful bargains on vegetables close to wilting, fruit that was at its ripest, and bread about to go stale. Aunt Millie bought a whole bag of day-old rolls, jelly buns, and doughnuts for a dime, a loaf of crushed bread and a box of broken cookies for a nickel each, two dented cans of peaches for six cents, and a huge bag of bruised apples for a quarter.

Kit was impressed by Aunt Millie's money-saving cleverness. Yet for some reason, Kit squirmed. *Everyone in this store must know my family's too poor to pay full prices,* she thought. Aunt Millie counted every penny of her change. When the grocer sighed impatiently and the people waiting in line craned their heads around to see what was taking so long, Kit went hot with self-consciousness.

As they walked home, Aunt Millie said, "You're very quiet, Margaret Mildred. Where's what Shakespeare would call my 'merry lark'?"

Kit spoke slowly. "Aunt Millie," she said, "do you ever feel funny about . . . you know . . . having to buy crushed bread and broken cookies and all?"

"Everything we bought's perfectly good," said Aunt Millie. "It may not *look* perfect, but none of it's rotten or spoiled. It'll taste fine, you'll see."

"I meant," Kit faltered, "it's . . . hard to be poor in front of people."

"Being poor is nothing to be ashamed of," said Aunt Millie stoutly, "especially these days, with so many folks in the same boat."

Kit shook herself. How silly she was being! Of course Aunt Millie was right. Kit knew she should be proud of Aunt Millie's thrifty ideas. Wasn't that the whole point of the *Almanac*? Kit turned her thoughts to her book. *Which section should I put these new grocery shopping ideas in?* she wondered. *"Cooking" or "Miscellaneous Savings"?*

Grace

uess what?" Stirling asked Kit one afternoon as she was scouring out the bathtub. "We're going to have to add a new section to the *Almanac*."

"What'll it be?" asked Kit.

"Come downstairs," Stirling said, smiling. "You'll see."

Kit finished her cleaning and then went downstairs. The front door was open. Mother, Dad, Stirling, and Aunt Millie were standing outside, gathered around a wooden crate.

Dad grinned at Aunt Millie. "You've outdone yourself this time," he said.

Kit gasped. The crate was full of chickens! Live, squawking, white-feathered chickens! Kit knelt next to the crate. "Are they ours?" she asked.

"Yes, ma'am," said Aunt Millie. "I swapped for them. Remember that bag of apples? I cut out the bruises, made pies, and traded them."

"You swapped pies for chickens?" asked Dad.

"Well, I threw in a few other things, too," said Aunt Millie.

"Are we . . . are we going to *eat* the chickens?" asked Kit, who had already fallen in love with the fat, noisy, *cluck-cluck-clucking* birds.

"Heavens no!" said Aunt Millie. "We're going to sell their eggs."

"*Who's* going to sell their eggs?" asked Mother.

Aunt Millie put one hand on Kit's shoulder and the other on Stirling's shoulder. "My partners here," she said, "will go door-to-door selling the eggs."

Mother looked dismayed. "The children will be selling eggs to our neighbors?" she asked. "As if they were . . . *peddlers?*"

"Folks are always glad to buy fresh eggs," said Aunt Millie. She turned to Kit and Stirling. "Come on, partners. Let's get these hens settled. The sooner they are settled, the sooner they'll lay eggs, and the sooner we'll be in business."

Stirling looked sideways at Kit. "'Chickens,'" he murmured.

Kit grinned and nodded. That would be the name of the newest section of *Aunt Millie's Waste-Not, Want-Not Almanac*.

Dad built a chicken coop behind the garage. Mother had put her foot down and insisted that the chicken coop must not be visible from the house. Of course, it was still possible to hear and often *smell* the chickens from the house. Kit knew that this distressed Mother, who was not happy about the chickens in the first place. Kit heard her say to Dad, "I do wish Miss Mildred had asked us before she hatched this chickens-and-eggs idea."

Everyone else was delighted with the chickens, especially Kit herself. The chickens weren't very smart, but they were cheerful. They made Kit laugh the way they clucked so excitedly all day long. Kit enjoyed feeding them. She scooped out handfuls of feed from the big cloth feed sack and scattered it on the ground. Often, as she fed the chickens, Kit felt like a farm girl living out in the country long, long ago.

Sometimes it seemed to Kit that she was leading

two completely different lives. One life was at home
with Aunt Millie and her quirky, economical, country
ways that Kit wrote about in the *Almanac*. Her other
life, at school, was entirely separate. Except for Ruthie
and Stirling, none of Kit's classmates knew anything
about her "waste-not, want-not" life at home. Kit wondered what they'd think if they did.

❀

The weather, in spring's fickle way, turned cold
and rainy. The rain was good news for the vegetable
patch, which had a crew cut of green sprouts. But it
was not good news for Kit and Stirling, who were
planning to go on their very first egg-selling expedi-
tion this very afternoon. The rain was not good news
for Mother and Mrs. Howard, either, because for the
first time in a long time, the garden club ladies were
coming for a meeting.

Inviting the garden club ladies had been another
of Aunt Millie's ideas. Mother was reluctant. She
liked things to be *just so* for the garden club meetings. Of course, there had been no money or time for
such fussing since Dad lost his job and the boarders

arrived. The meetings could never again be as fancy
or elaborate as those in the old days. For one thing,
Mother had sold a great deal of her good silver. But
Aunt Millie had insisted they could still have a fine
party. "You leave it to me," she had said. "I'll use energy instead of money."

And sure enough, when Kit saw the room set up
for the party, she knew that Aunt Millie had pulled
off another one of her amazing surprises. She had
washed the best linen tablecloth and napkins to make
them dazzling white, then starched and ironed them
into stiff perfection. She had polished the one remain-
ing silver candleholder until it gleamed. She made
peach pies and apple pies that were works of art. No
one would know the peaches came out of dented
cans and the apples were bruised. And no one would
ever guess that her dainty tea sandwiches were made
of crushed bread with the crusts cut off and wilted
watercress she'd made crisp by soaking it in cold
water overnight. Aunt Millie had dusted, polished,
and swept the house till it shone, despite the gloomy
weather outside.

Mother and Mrs. Howard, who was quite perked

up by the idea of the party, placed a gorgeous bouquet of irises from the garden on the table. Then Mother stood back to survey the whole room.

"Miss Mildred," said Mother with a big, genuine smile. "Thank you very much for everything you've done. It all looks beautiful."

"It's just a matter of making the best of what you've got," said Aunt Millie. She shooed Mother out of the room, saying, "You skedaddle now. Go get *yourself* beautiful for your ladies." Then Aunt Millie turned to Kit and Stirling. "You two skedaddle, too. Go sell those eggs. When you're done, come see me. I'll have some goodies for you from the party."

So Kit and Stirling went out into the rain. Kit pulled the wagon while Stirling kept an eye on the eggs. Aunt Millie had divided them into groups of six, which she had wrapped carefully in newspaper so that they wouldn't crack or break. It was raining so hard that the newspaper was soon soggy. Kit tried not to jiggle the wagon as they walked around the corner and up the sidewalk to the first house.

Kit rang the doorbell.

"Yes?" asked the lady who came to the door.

"Would you like to buy some eggs?" Kit asked.

"How much . . . ?" the lady began. She stopped and stared at Kit. "Why, aren't you the little Kittredge girl, Margaret Kittredge's daughter?" she asked, peering through the rain. "What are *you* doing selling eggs? Wherever did you get them?"

The lady's questions embarrassed Kit. She swallowed hard and said, "They're from our chickens. They're twenty-five cents a dozen."

"*Your* chickens?" asked the lady. "It's come to that? Your family is raising chickens? In your yard?"

Kit felt hot, the way she had in the grocery store. The lady made it sound as if her family had lost all dignity and sunk into humiliating poverty.

Stirling glanced at Kit, then saved the situation by speaking up boldly. "Yes, the chickens live right around the corner," he said. "So you know these eggs are good and fresh. How many do you want?"

"Well!" said the lady. "I'll take a dozen." She carefully counted out her money, took the eggs, and closed the door.

Kit turned to Stirling. "Let's go to a street farther away," she said.

"Okay," said Stirling. Kit could tell by the look in his gray eyes that he knew why she wanted to go where no one knew her.

It was easy to sell the eggs, just as Aunt Millie had said it would be. People were pleased to buy fresh eggs delivered right to their doors at a price slightly lower than the price in the store. Kit soon had one dollar and twenty-five cents in her pocket. And yet, as she and Stirling walked home, Kit felt tired and disheartened. She knew she shouldn't have been ashamed by the first lady's questions, but she was, all the same. A drop of rain dripped off the end of her nose. Kit swiped it with her hand, which was also wet. Everything was miserable and discouraging because of the leaden sky and dreary rain. Then, on the sidewalk ahead, Kit saw a muddy brown lump. She stopped.

"What is it?" asked Stirling.

Kit knelt down next to the lump. "It's a dog," she said, gently touching one wet, furry ear. "A poor, starving, pitiful dog." Attached to a string around the dog's neck was a soggy piece of paper with a message on it. The rain had blurred the writing so that the words had inky tears dripping from them, but Kit could read: *Can't feed her anymore.*

The dog sighed, and looked at Kit with the saddest eyes she'd ever seen. The look went straight to Kit's heart, making her forget all about her own hurt feelings. "Stirling, this dog's been abandoned," she said. "We've got to bring her home and feed her."

Stirling didn't hesitate. "Let's put her in the wagon," he said. "Aunt Millie will know how to save her."

"Come on, old girl," Kit said softly as she and Stirling awkwardly lifted the dog into the wagon. The poor creature looked like a bag of bones and fur with its short hind legs folded beneath its stomach, its long, forlorn face resting on its muddy front paws, and its droopy ears puddled around its head. The dog did not move or whimper the whole time Kit pulled the wagon home. It did not even lift its head when Kit stopped outside the screen door.

Stirling went into the kitchen and brought Aunt Millie outside.

"You've got to help, Aunt Millie," said Kit. "We think she's starving."

"Heavenly day!" said Aunt Millie. She bent down

to examine the dog. "You children did the right thing,
rescuing this poor dog. She's a sorrowful sight now,
and I don't suppose she'll ever be a beauty, but she's a
fine old hound. Not a thing wrong with her that food
and loving care won't cure. She'll be a good guard dog
for us and will more than earn her keep." Aunt Millie
stood up and said briskly, "Put her in the garage. Keep
her there until your mother's party is over. I'll rustle up
some scraps and bring them out to you as soon as I can.
Later, we'll bathe her."

As Kit and Stirling pulled the wagon to the garage,
several things happened at once. The rain stopped, the
clouds parted, and the sun shone at last. Mother and
the garden club ladies came outside. They stood on the
terrace to admire the azaleas, which looked heavenly
with the raindrops sparkling on their delicate, colorful petals. The chickens were drawn outside by the
sunshine, too. They emerged from their coop, strutting
and clucking with enthusiasm, to peck in the mud for
worms brought up by the rain.

At the sound of the chickens, the dog suddenly
lifted its nose and sniffed the air. To Kit and Stirling's
astonishment, the dog threw back its head and let loose

a bloodcurdling howl. The ladies screeched, the chickens squawked, and the dog bolted out of the wagon and took off toward the chickens like a shot, barking wildly. Its lope was ungainly and awkward, but it was amazingly fast. Before anyone knew what was happening, the dog had chased some of the chickens across the lawn and onto the terrace, right into the middle of the ladies! The ladies protested as loudly as the chickens as the dog herded them all into the dining room, closely followed by Kit and Stirling.

Feathers flew. Kit chased the chickens and the dog around the tea table, trying to call to the dog above the ladies' shrieks. Dad, Charlie, and some of the boarders thundered down the stairs shouting, "What's going on?" Aunt Millie heard the racket and barreled out of the kitchen, flapping her apron at the chickens and shouting instructions to Kit.

Finally, Kit took a flying leap and tackled the dog. In so doing, she jostled the table. The china rattled like chattering teeth. The centerpiece of flowers rocked wildly. The candleholder tottered, fell over, then crashed to the floor. Somehow, Aunt Millie and Stirling shooed the chickens, who were still clucking indignantly, outside. Kit dragged the dog into the kitchen. She didn't dare take it outside until the chickens were safely shut up in their coop.

The calamity was over, but the party was ruined. The ladies scooped up their gloves and purses, said hurried thank-yous and good-byes to Mother, and scurried home. The house was suddenly quiet.

"I'm so sorry," said Kit when Mother came into the kitchen.

"You should apologize to Miss Mildred," said Mother wearily. "She's the one who worked so hard to make the party beautiful." Mother shook her head. "For myself, I don't know whether to laugh or cry. I've never seen such a disaster in all my life. Where on earth did that filthy dog come from?"

"Aunt Millie says—" Kit began, but Mother held up her hand.

"Stop," she said. "Don't bother telling me. I can guess. The dog is one of Miss Mildred's rescue projects." She sighed. "I am grateful for all her hard work these past weeks. But I'm at my wit's end! My home has not been my own since . . ." Mother didn't finish her sentence, but she didn't need to. Kit knew that she was going to say "since Miss Mildred came."

Mother put her hands on her hips and leaned forward. "You," she said to the dog, "smell. But Miss Mildred can never resist a hopeless cause, so I guess we're stuck with you. Well, I hope you're happy, dog. It's thanks to you that my garden club party was the party to end all parties."

The party to end all parties, thought Kit. *Oh dear.*

❇

After Kit and Aunt Millie cleaned up the party mess, they bathed and fed the dog. Then they went upstairs to the attic together. Kit brought the dog along. She was afraid to let the dog out of her sight for fear of what the animal might do! Of course, the dog looked sweetly peaceful and serene now. It rested its head on Kit's knee and looked up at Kit with trusting, loving eyes.

"Aunt Millie," said Kit, "I'm sorry the dog ruined the party."

"Nothing was broken," said Aunt Millie. "And the ladies had already eaten all the refreshments, so nothing was wasted. The dog just provided a rather spectacular ending to the party."

"Mother said it was the party to end all parties,"
said Kit. She sighed deeply.

"There now, Margaret Mildred," Aunt Millie said.
"'Sigh no more,' as Shakespeare would say. Tell me
what's on your mind."

Kit went to her desk and took the picture of the
Robin Hood birthday party out of the drawer. She
showed it to Aunt Millie. "I really wanted a birthday
party this year," she said. "I knew it couldn't be as fancy
as the one in this picture, and I probably shouldn't
want one at all. But Stirling and Ruthie said that want-
ing was the same as hoping, and that hope is always
good." Kit sighed again, in spite of Shakespeare. "They
were wrong. After what happened today, there's absolutely no chance that there will be any party for me. I
was stupid to hope."

"Well!" said Aunt Millie crisply. "I happen to agree
with Ruthie and Stirling. I hate to give up on *anything*.
Not hopes, not parties . . ." She smiled. "Not even a
homely creature like this dog you found who trips over
her own feet and causes all kinds of trouble!"

Aunt Millie's words made Kit feel better. She

hugged the dog. "What should I call her?" she asked.

"There's only one name for a dog as clumsy and ungraceful as that," said Aunt Millie.

"What is it?" asked Kit.

"Grace," said Aunt Millie.

So Grace it was.

Penny-Pincher Party

t seemed, after all, that Grace had only been trying to express how happy she was to meet the chickens. Much to everyone's surprise, Grace soon became the chickens' best friend. She followed Kit around when Kit fed the chickens, and spent most of her day asleep outside their coop. That was just as well, because there she was out of Mother's sight. Whenever Kit came outside to be sure the chickens had enough water, Grace opened one eye, thumped her tail lazily, then went back to sleep. The chickens forgave and accepted Grace. They went about the business of eating their feed, clucking, and laying their eggs with Grace for company.

"These chickens are the fattest and finest chickens in Cincinnati," Aunt Millie said one day when she and Kit were feeding them.

"They should be," said Kit, folding up an empty feed sack, "considering all the feed they eat." Kit didn't mean to sound critical of the chickens. She still liked *them* even if she did dislike selling their eggs.

"I'll take that feed sack," said Aunt Millie. "I have something special in mind for it."

I wonder what? thought Kit as she handed Aunt Millie the big, flowered sack. *Dish towels? Pillowcases? No matter what, it'll be something new for the "Sewing" section of Aunt Millie's Waste-Not, Want-Not Almanac!*

All of the sections of the *Almanac* were more and more filled in. Kit, Ruthie, and Stirling had carefully recorded Aunt Millie's recipe for pickling "dilly beans," the early green beans from the vegetable patch. They'd also written her advice about storing winter woolen blankets and coats in mothballs for the summer. How Kit wished she could put away her winter woolen school clothes, too! But her spring clothes from last year did not fit her, and there was no money to buy new clothes. So, despite the fact that the weather was growing warmer, Kit had to wear heavy, uncomfortable winter clothes to school. As soon as she came home to work in the garden, she put on the raggy, baggy old overalls she had inherited from Charlie. When Kit kicked off her shoes and peeled off her socks and worked barefoot in the vegetable patch, she felt like a different person— one her classmates wouldn't even recognize.

The day before Kit's birthday was the warmest day yet. Kit could feel sweat prickling the back of her neck under her wool collar as she walked to school with Stirling and Ruthie, and it was only eight o'clock in the morning!

By afternoon Kit's clothes felt so tight and itchy that she could hardly pay attention to her teacher, Mr. Fisher. The classroom was stuffy even with the windows open, and everyone else seemed restless, too. The students all wiggled in their seats. There was lots of whispering and foot shuffling.

"Boys and girls!" Mr. Fisher said sharply. "Quiet!"

At that moment, the door to the classroom swung open. The students spun around to see who it was. When they did, they stared.

Kit gasped. It was Aunt Millie!

A low ripple of giggles swept through the classroom. Kit looked at Aunt Millie through her classmates' eyes and understood why they were giggling.

Aunt Millie did look peculiar. She was wearing her clean but faded workaday dress, and her Sunday-best hat and shoes. Her hair wisped out from under her hat. Her cheeks were ruddier than usual.

"Mr. Fisher," she said in her twangy voice, "I'm Margaret Mildred Kittredge's Aunt Millie, and I'd like to speak to your class."

"Uh, certainly," Mr. Fisher said. "Go ahead."

Aunt Millie beamed at Kit as she strode to the front of the classroom. Kit tried hard to smile back at Aunt Millie, but she couldn't. The classroom hissed with whispers. Roger, the boy behind Kit, poked her back. "That's your aunt?" he asked. "She looks like she just got off the farm."

Kit flushed with anger—and embarrassment. Roger was right. The way Aunt Millie looked was fine at home, but it was all wrong here in front of Kit's class-mates. *Oh, why did Aunt Millie come here?* she wondered.

"I've come today to invite all of you to a birthday party for Margaret Mildred," Aunt Millie said. "It'll be after school tomorrow at our house, and it'll be a jim-dandy."

Jim-dandy? Some of the students laughed and

repeated Aunt Millie's unfamiliar expression to one another in giggled whispers.

This is terrible, thought Kit. She stiffened as Aunt Millie went on. "I've been teaching Margaret Mildred and her friends lots of ways to save money and have fun at the same time," Aunt Millie said. "They've enjoyed it, and I bet all of you would, too. So come to our Penny-Pincher Party tomorrow. You can have beans out of our vegetable patch. I'll show you how to make a salad out of dandelion greens, and you can feed the chickens."

Chickens! The students exploded in merriment. They flapped their arms as if they were chicken wings. Some of the girls and boys made clucking sounds, and Roger crowed like a rooster.

Kit was so mortified she wished she could disappear and never be seen again. But Aunt Millie did not seem the least bit disturbed by the students' antics. "I'll even show you how to make bloomers out of a flour sack!" she said.

Bloomers! Now the students were laughing out loud. Aunt Millie laughed, too, as if they were all in on a wonderful joke together.

She doesn't even realize they are making fun of her! Kit thought. *She doesn't know that now they will make fun of* ***me.*** *Oh, how I wish she had never come!* Kit thought of how she'd felt at the grocery store, and selling the eggs. *It was bad enough to be embarrassed in front of strangers. This is much, much worse.*

"Well!" said Mr. Fisher to Aunt Millie. "Thank you!" He turned to Kit. "Perhaps you'd like to escort your aunt to the door," he said.

Kit stood up. Her knees were wobbly, and she was so red in the face, she felt as if she were on fire. Silently, she led Aunt Millie through the halls to the front door of the school.

"Margaret Mildred," asked Aunt Millie, "whatever is the matter?"

Kit bit her lip and looked at her shoes. She was too angry to look Aunt Millie in the eyes.

"Don't you *like* the idea of the Penny-Pincher Party?" Aunt Millie asked.

"No," said Kit in a raspy whisper. She looked up at Aunt Millie with eyes that were full of hot tears. "I don't. I hate it. It's . . . *embarrassing.* Why did you tell everyone at school about the things we do at home?

That's private. I don't want my friends to know how poor we are. I never want them to *see* it. Oh, I wish . . . I wish you had never come!"

Aunt Millie stepped back. "Ah," she said softly. "I see." She turned away from Kit. "I'm sorry, dear child," she said. Then she left.

❈

Kit, Ruthie, and Stirling did not talk as they walked home together after school. As soon as Kit got to her house, she ran upstairs to her room and flung herself facedown on her bed. All the burning tears she had bottled up inside came pouring out. Kit cried and cried. Soon her pillow was hot and damp from her tears and her sweat.

A soothing breeze blew in the window and lifted the hair stuck to the back of Kit's neck. Kit raised her head so that the breeze could cool her face. Suddenly, she sat up. Hanging in front of the window, fluttering gently on the breeze, was a dress. It was simple and flowery, springy and *beautiful*. Kit stood up, pulled off her too-heavy winter clothes, and slipped the dress on. It felt so cool and light and airy, she felt as if she could fly. Kit smoothed the front of the dress with her hands and looked at the material. It was then that she realized: the dress was made out of a chicken-feed sack. It was another one of Aunt Millie's magical transformations.

Kit sat down hard on the bed. *Oh, Aunt Millie!* she thought. *How could I have spoken to you the way I did at school? How could I have been ashamed of you? How could I have been so wrong?*

Kit ran downstairs as fast as she could and found Mother and Dad in the kitchen. "Where's Aunt Millie?" she asked.

"Kit, sweetheart, Aunt Millie asked us to say good-bye to you for her," said Dad. "She decided to go home on the four-thirty train today."

"She's *gone*?" wailed Kit. "Oh, it's all my fault." Hurriedly, Kit told Mother and Dad what had happened at school. "But now I see how wrong I was. Please, we've got to stop her. You don't want her to go back to Kentucky, do you?"

Dad looked at Mother with a question in his eyes. Suddenly, Mother smiled. "If we hurry," she said, "we can catch her before she gets on the train."

❄

The train station was huge, noisy, and full of people.
But Kit spotted Aunt Millie right away. She was sitting
perfectly straight with her suitcase by her side, reading
a book of Shakespeare's poems. Kit ran to her.

"Aunt Millie!" Kit said breathlessly. "I'm so sorry!
Please don't go."

Mother and Dad came up behind Kit. "We need
you, Miss Mildred," said Mother. "We can't get along
without you."

"Won't you come back with us?" asked Dad.

Aunt Millie smiled a small smile. "No, my dears,"
she said. "You've been very kind, putting up with me
and my bossiness. But I can see that my country ways
don't fit here in the city. For you they are . . ." She gave
Kit a kindly, forgiving look, then said, "For you they
are embarrassing." Then she spoke briskly. "No, it's
time for me to go, and take my ideas with me."

Kit sat down next to Aunt Millie. Gently, she took
Aunt Millie's book out of her hands and put another
book in its place. It was the *Waste-Not, Want-Not
Almanac*. "Look," Kit said earnestly, turning the pages
so that Aunt Millie could see. "Stirling and Ruthie and
I made this. It's full of your ideas. We liked them so

much, we put them in this book so we'd never forget them."

"Hea-ven-ly day!" said Aunt Millie in a long, drawn-out, surprised whisper. She touched the dandelion green Ruthie had glued to a page, studied Stirling's sketch of the chickens, and smiled at Kit's list of grocery shopping tips. When she looked up at Kit, Mother, and Dad, her eyes were bright.

"I hope you'll come home, Aunt Millie," said Kit, "and teach all my friends your ideas, too, at the Penny-Pincher Party."

Aunt Millie stood up and held out her hand to Kit. "'Let's away,'" she said, quoting Shakespeare in her old, lively way.

Dad carried her suitcase and Mother carried her basket, because Aunt Millie's hands were full. She was holding Kit's hand in one of her hands, and carrying the *Waste-Not, Want-Not Almanac* in the other.

❀

The Penny-Pincher Party was the best birthday party Kit had ever had. Kit's classmates agreed afterward that it was the best birthday party *anyone* had ever had.

Aunt Millie had planned the whole party, but everyone helped. Stirling made paper party hats for all the guests, including Grace, who appeared to be under the impression that the party was in *her* honor. She trotted from guest to guest and leaned up against each one, allowing the chance to pet her. While Mr. Peck played his bass fiddle, Mr. and Mrs. Bell taught the children to square-dance and Miss Hart and Miss Finney taught them to sing "My Darling Clementine." The ragman was there, and he and Dad gave the children rides on his horse. Charlie took pictures of them with his camera. Aunt Millie's friend the butcher helped the children cook hot dogs on sticks over a fire, and Mrs. Howard and Mother taught the children to make flower crowns and necklaces.

The children liked Aunt Millie's penny-pincher lessons best of all. Aunt Millie taught them how to pick the most tender dandelion greens to make a salad. She showed them how to feed the chickens and collect their eggs. She brought out a flour sack full of sunflower seeds and taught the children how to plant, water, and weed. "Remember," she said, quoting Shakespeare, "'sweet flowers take time, weeds make haste.'"

When the flour sack was empty, Aunt Millie held it up. "Well," she said, with a twinkle in her eye. "Look at this. An empty cloth sack. Would you like me to show you how to make bloomers out of this?"

"Yes!" shouted all the children, including Kit. They laughed, and Kit realized that even in school, they had been laughing in delight at the idea, not meanly. They were as enchanted by Aunt Millie as Kit and Stirling and Ruthie had been.

"You are so lucky, Kit," sighed Ruthie. "This is a wonderful party." The sun had set. The yard was lit with lanterns Aunt Millie had saved from a trash pile and repaired. The lanterns had candles inside them, and they swayed in the soft evening breeze so that their light danced across the grass. Kit, Ruthie, and Stirling were sitting together eating the chocolate roll cake Aunt Millie had made. Ruthie asked, "Do you mind that it's not a Robin Hood party?"

"You know, in a way it *is* a Robin Hood party," Kit said, "because Aunt Millie reminds me of Robin Hood. She doesn't rob from the rich to give to the poor. But she scrimps and saves and then whatever she has, she gives away. She's thrifty in order to be generous." Kit spread out her arms. "Look at this party she's created for all of us, even after I was terrible to her about it."

"How *did* you convince her not to leave?" asked Stirling.

Kit grinned. "How do you think?" she asked.

Ruthie and Stirling both looked at Kit with sparkling eyes. "You showed her the *Almanac!*" they said together.

"Yup," said Kit, *"Aunt Millie's Waste-Not, Want-Not Almanac,* with all her great ideas inside."

"You know," said Stirling, "I think we should add a new section."

"Right!" said Ruthie. "We could call it 'Having a Penny-Pincher Party.'"

"Or maybe," said Kit, "'How to Have a Very Happy Birthday.'"

Stuck

o Kit's delight, Aunt Millie stayed with the Kittredges all summer. Kit was especially glad Aunt Millie was there after Charlie left. In June, he took a train to faraway Montana to work for the Civilian Conservation Corps, which was a program started by President Roosevelt to provide jobs for young men who were out of work because of the Depression.

Kit was thrilled for Charlie, but she missed him terribly. She missed playing catch with him in the backyard. She missed his jokes, his big, guffawing laugh, and the way he took the stairs two at a time. She wrote lots of newspapers to keep him posted on all the news from home, and she saved every one of his letters so that she could read them whenever she got too lonely. Kit could tell that Mother, Dad, and Aunt Millie missed

Charlie, too. She thought that even Grace seemed a
little mopey without him.

Now it was a hot, sticky, boring afternoon in Au-
gust, and it seemed to Kit that her brother had been
gone for ages. So when she checked the mailbox and
saw a thick envelope with Charlie's handwriting on the
front, she whooped with joy.

Kit flew into the kitchen waving the envelope over
her head. "Look, everybody!" she shouted. "It's from
Charlie!" Kit's mother, dad, and Aunt Millie gathered
around her eagerly. "Here, Dad," Kit said. "You read it."

Mr. Kittredge dried his hands on the dish towel
wrapped around his waist before he took the letter. The
kitchen was steamy because the grownups were steril-
izing glass jars in boiling water to prepare them for
jams and preserves.

"'Dear Folks,'" Dad read aloud. "'I'm sitting on a
patch of snow . . .'"

"Snow!" exclaimed Kit enviously.

"Shh!" shushed Mother and Aunt Millie.

Dad continued, "'. . . on a mountaintop here in
Glacier National Park. There's nothing but blue sky
and pine trees around me. This week, we're working

on a stone wall next to a road called 'Going-to-the-Sun Highway.' It's hard, but all of us fellows are glad to have work to do. We have fun, too. I've told my baseball team that my kid sister Kit is the best catcher in Cincinnati! Well, break time's over. I'll write again soon. I miss you. I wish all of you could see how pretty Montana is. Love, Charlie.'"

For a moment after Dad finished reading, everyone just stood there grinning. It was as if Charlie had sent a brisk mountain breeze in his letter, a breeze that blew all the way from Glacier Park to stir the stifling air in the kitchen, refresh everyone, and lift their spirits.

"This is for you, Kit," said Dad. He handed Kit a photo of Charlie in a group of young men. They were in a forest, smiling broadly at the camera.

Kit saw a note on the back. "'Hey, Squirt!'" she read aloud. "'I thought you'd like this photo of me and my CCC buddies. Write and tell me what you're up to. XO, Charlie.'" Kit rose on her toes in delight. She loved writing! "I'll go make one of my newspapers for Charlie right now," she announced. She slipped the photo into her pocket and took off flying toward the hall.

"Kit!" said Mother. "Have you finished your chores?"

Kit crash-landed to a stop. "No," she admitted,
"but—"

"Please do, dear," said Mother, "before you do anything else."

Aunt Millie added, "And please give the chickens
fresh water. They'll be thirsty on a hot day like today."

Kit scowled, but none of the grownups noticed.
They'd already turned back to their work. Clouds of
steam rose from the pots on the stove, and the glass jars
clinked and clanked in the boiling water.

"'Double, double toil and trouble; Fire burn and
cauldron bubble,'" said Aunt Millie cheerfully, wiping
her foggy eyeglasses on her apron.

Kit knew Aunt Millie was quoting the witches in a
play by Shakespeare called *Macbeth*. Right now, Kit felt
as low-down as a mean witch. She let the screen door
slam shut behind her and stalked over to the chicken
pen. The chickens usually greeted her with energetic
squawking. But today they were under a listless spell
because of the heat. They ignored Kit and didn't bother
to cluck their thanks when she filled their water pan.

I'm just a drudge, Kit grumbled to herself, feeling
cross that even the chickens seemed to take her for

granted. She picked up her broom and went back to
work beating the rug hung over the clothesline. *Mop,
sweep, scrub, polish, do the laundry, wash the dishes, feed the
chickens, weed the garden—my chores never end!*

Dust and dirt billowed up off the rug and stuck
to Kit's sweaty face and arms so that she was soon as
spotty as an old brown toad. She kicked off her sandals,
which, like all of her clothes, were too small. But free-
ing her feet did not cheer her up. The more Kit thought
about her situation, the crosser she became. She'd *never*
have time to write a newspaper for Charlie. After beating the rug, she was supposed to help Dad clean out
the gutters. After that, it would be time to help Mother
cook and serve dinner. And after dinner, there'd be the
dishes to wash, dry, and put away.

Kit whacked the rug harder than was strictly
necessary.

"Wow," said Stirling, crossing the yard toward Kit.
"I wish your broom was a bat and the rug was a ball.
That would have been a home run."

"And *that*," Kit said grimly as she walloped the rug
again, "is as close as I'll get to swinging a baseball bat
this summer."

Dust from the rug surrounded Stirling like a dirty cloud, but he didn't budge. He stood patiently, waiting for Kit to explain why she was so grumpy. Kit's dog Grace ambled over. Grace liked to be wherever a conversation was going on. She plunked herself down and drooled on Kit's kicked-off sandals.

"We had a letter from Charlie," Kit said. "He sent me this." Kit took Charlie's photo out of her pocket and gave it to Stirling. "Read the back."

Stirling did. Then he said, "Let's go make him a newspaper."

"I can't!" Kit exploded. "I have to do my dumb chores!"

Kit knew it was unfair to snap at Stirling. Chores weren't *his* fault. Besides, he worked hard, too. At the beginning of the summer, he'd surprised everyone by up and getting himself a job selling newspapers on a street corner. Stirling still looked like a pip-squeak, but he acted sturdier and more sure of himself. Kit thought it was because he had a real job out in the world and was earning money—just like Charlie, who sent home twenty-five of the thirty dollars he earned through the CCC every month.

"Sorry you can't write a newspaper for Charlie," said Stirling.

"Well, what would I write about anyway?" said Kit, putting the photo back in her pocket. "Dusting? The laundry? I'm not doing anything exciting. Charlie's the one who's having an adventure." Kit sighed and leaned on her broom. "The truth is," she admitted, "I'm jealous of Charlie." Lucky Charlie was living in a place where there were mountain peaks and hidden valleys, cool blue lakes and dark green pines, rushing streams and thundering waterfalls. By contrast, Kit's life was flat, colorless, and humdrum. "I wish *I* could have an adventure," she said. "I'm tired of doing the same old chores. I feel so bogged down, so *stuck*. I'd like to fly away and escape."

"In that case," said Stirling, "I don't wish your broom was a baseball bat. I wish it was a witch's broom."

Kit laughed in spite of herself. She straddled the broom and pretended to try to take off but remained, of course, solidly planted on the ground. "I give up," she said. "Looks like my broom's stuck, too."

❄

Kit slapped at a mosquito. Too late. Now there'd be
a bite on her neck, which was already sunburned and
itchy with sweat.

It was a few days later. Kit was in the vegetable garden, moving slowly between rows of tomato plants and
picking the ripest tomatoes off the vines. Aunt Millie
had declared today tomato harvest day. She'd decided
that most of the tomatoes were ready to be preserved,
and she did not want to waste one tomato—or one
minute, either. She had rousted everyone out of bed at
dawn and hurried them to work.

By now it was mid-morning. Kit and Stirling were
outside picking. Mother was in the kitchen stewing
and preserving. Dad was carrying jars of preserved
tomatoes to the basement. Aunt Millie buzzed back and
forth, inside and outside, bossing both pickers and pre-
servers. "We'll be glad for all this work come winter,"
she said happily. "Think of the money we'll save by eating food we've grown ourselves. And it'll remind us of
summer. When we eat these tomatoes, we'll remember
what Shakespeare calls 'summer's honey breath'!"

Kit and Stirling smiled at each other through the
tomato plants. They were both accustomed to the way

Aunt Millie quoted Shakespeare.

As usual, Aunt Millie and Shakespeare were quite
right. The air *did* feel like honey—liquid, heavy, and
sticky. Even so, Kit was grateful to be outdoors. The day
before she'd practically melted in the suffocating kitchen
helping Aunt Millie make peach jam. Kit had stirred
the pot of thick goo on the stove until her hand was
glued to the spoon with peach juice and her feet were
pasted to the floor with jam. Today, in the garden, there
was at least a sluggish breeze rustling the limp leaves
every so often. The tomatoes glowed red and were so
plump they seemed about to burst their smooth skins.
Each one had a satisfying heft when Kit held it in her
hand. Her basket was heavy when she stood up and
carried it to Aunt Millie, who took it inside.

Kit had knelt down and gone back to picking when
Grace barked a friendly bark. Grace was supposed to be
a guard dog, but she seemed to think that anyone who
came to the house had come only to admire *her* and
therefore should be welcomed politely. Kit poked her
head up above the tomatoes.

"Hey," said someone.

Kit turned and saw a stranger standing at the edge

of the garden. It was a teenage boy in a dusty cap and stained, baggy, roughly patched trousers.

"Hey, yourself," Kit said.

Now Stirling raised his head, too. The teenage boy grinned such a big, wide grin that Kit and Stirling had to smile back. Kit knew he was a hobo. He had the same scruffy, scrawny look as all the hoboes and tramps who came to the house looking for a handout or a job to do in return for food.

The boy bent down to scratch Grace's back. He nodded toward the garden. "The tomatoes look good," he said. Just then the screen door opened and Aunt Millie came out. The boy's grin disappeared. He shot up straight, pulled his cap off, and pushed his shaggy, dark hair out of his eyes. "How do, ma'am," he said. His voice was respectful and a little wary. He sounded as if he half expected Aunt Millie to shoo him away.

But Kit knew Aunt Millie would never shoo away a stray *dog*, much less a stray boy. "What can I do for you, son?" Aunt Millie asked.

"Well, ma'am," said the boy. "I was just saying to the young lady yonder what a good crop of tomatoes you've got. Your string beans are ready to be picked, too. I'd be glad to help. Looks like maybe you could use a hand."

"Looks like maybe *you* could use a bite to eat," said Aunt Millie. "You're as skinny as a string bean yourself!"

The boy grinned his wide, wonderful grin again. "I'd be obliged," he said. "But not until after I work."

Aunt Millie smiled. "What's your name, son?" she asked.

"William Shepherd," answered the boy. "But nowadays, most folks call me Texas Will, or just plain Will."

"All right, just plain Will," said Aunt Millie. She handed him an empty basket. "You can help Kit and Stirling with the picking. Mind, there won't be any pay in it for you. None but lunch, anyway."

"That'll do fine, ma'am," said Will. He bent over a tomato plant and went straight to work.

"I'll tell the folks inside there'll be one more for lunch," said Aunt Millie. She went back into the kitchen.

Kit was burning with curiosity about Will. She had hundreds of questions to ask him. Also, she wanted to hear Will talk more. She liked the way he pronounced his name "wheel" and called Aunt Millie "may-um."

"Are you from Texas?" Kit asked.

"Yep," Will answered without stopping his work.

"How'd you get as far as Cincinnati?" Stirling asked.

"Riding the rails, mostly," said Will. "Hopping freights. I ride freight trains for free by jumping into empty boxcars."

"Aren't you kind of young?" Kit asked. "To be a hobo, I mean."

"I'm fifteen," said Will. "There are lots of hoboes my age, some even younger." He glanced at Kit. "Girls not much older than you ride the rails."

"They do?" Kit asked, fascinated.

"Yep," said Will.

Gosh! thought Kit. *What a life that must be. Very exciting—and very **unstuck**!*

Just Plain Will

Will was a quick, quiet worker. With his help, all the ripest tomatoes were picked by lunchtime. Mother brought a tray of sandwiches outside, and Dad brought a pitcher of milk so that they could have lunch on the shady back porch. Will looked at the sandwiches as if he could devour them all. Kit knew how he felt. She was always hungry herself. Mother often teased that Kit was eating them out of house and home! But before they could eat, Aunt Millie brought out a basin of hot water, a bar of soap, and a hand towel.

"Wash up, children," she ordered Kit, Stirling, and Will.

Kit and Stirling washed quickly. But Will pushed up his sleeves, plunged his hands into the hot water, and sighed with pleasure. He lathered up his hands, cupped them, and scooped up handful after handful of water to wash his face, letting the warm, soapy water run down his neck. Then he scrubbed his arms up to his elbows and dried off with the towel. Water drops glistened on his hair. Kit realized soap and hot water were luxuries hoboes like Will probably didn't often see.

"You're a good worker, Will," said Aunt Millie as she filled his milk glass. "You know what you're doing in a garden."

"I ought to," said Will, with his winning grin. "My family had a farm back in Texas."

"Don't you miss your family?" asked Mother.

"I do, ma'am," answered Will. "And I miss the farm. It used to be beautiful. My father grew wheat. In the spring, the fields looked like a green ocean. Then hard times came. My father couldn't make any money selling his wheat. After that, it seemed like nature turned against us, because it never rained. The wheat dried up, dead and brown. It cracked under your feet when you walked through the fields, and the soil was nothing but dust." Will sighed. "A couple of big wind storms came and just blew the farm away. Scattered it. My family's gone, too. They packed up everything and left."

"How come you didn't go with them?" Kit asked
Will.

"Kit," Mother scolded gently. "That's a personal
question."

"It's all right, ma'am," said Will. He looked at Kit.
"See, my father is a proud man. It about killed him
when he lost the farm and couldn't feed us anymore. I
knew he hated having me see him brought so low. And
I knew I was one more mouth he couldn't feed, one
more pair of feet he couldn't buy shoes for. So when my
family packed up to leave Texas, I made up my mind to
go off on my own. I figured it was time for me to take
care of myself."

Kit understood. She felt guilty about her appetite
and about growing so much and so fast that she was
always needing bigger clothes and shoes, too. She felt
like Alice in Wonderland, who suddenly grew so big
she filled the house! Except that Alice's clothes grew,
too, which was very convenient. Kit's arms and legs
dangled out of most of her clothes as if she were a
gangly daddy longlegs. Kit thought Will was brave and
noble to have left his family so that he wasn't an expense to them anymore.

"Did you run away?" Stirling asked.

"Yep," said Will. "I've been most everywhere since then. I follow the crops. I went north to harvest potatoes in the fall, south to pick walnuts in the winter, and east to pick strawberries in the spring. Now I'm on my way west to Oregon for the apple harvest."

Dad spoke, and Kit heard something that sounded like envy in his voice. "You've seen a lot of country for someone your age," he said to Will.

"Yes, sir, and met a lot of people, too," said Will. "But none kinder than you folks." He stood up and put his cap back on his head. "Thank you for the fine lunch. I'll be on my way now."

Dad glanced at Mother and Aunt Millie. All three seemed to come to an agreement without saying a word.

Kit was happy when she heard Dad say, "Just a minute, Will. We'll be up to our elbows picking and preserving tomorrow, too. We'd be glad to have your help, if you'd like to stay. We can't pay you, but we can feed you and give you a place to sleep."

"I'll give you a haircut, too," said Aunt Millie. "You look like you haven't had one since you left home."

Will's grin lit his whole face. "Thanks," he said. "I'd like that. I'll stay."

"Good!" said Kit. "You can tell us about all the places you've been!"

❊

At first, Will was shy at dinner. But he soon grew comfortable and talkative. All the boarders liked him. Mother beamed at him, and Aunt Millie gave him extra-large portions of food. Dad, who was always interested in places he had never been, asked Kit to bring the atlas to the table. He opened the atlas to a map of the United States so that Will could show them where he was from in Texas and point out all the places he'd been before he came to Ohio. Kit found Glacier Park, Montana, on the map and told Will about Charlie and the work he was doing there with the CCC.

After dinner, Mr. Peck played his bass fiddle while Mrs. Bell played the piano, and Will taught them all to dance the Texas two-step.

"We haven't had that much fun since Charlie left," Kit said as she led Will outside, carrying a lantern, blankets, and a pillow. Will had chosen not to sleep in the house. "Where do you want these?" she asked. "In the garage? Or on the porch?"

"I'll sleep on the ground," said Will. "I'm not used to a roof anymore. Makes me feel too closed in."

"All right," said Kit. "Good night."

"Good night," said Will.

As Kit climbed up to her attic room, she thought that Will was wise to be outdoors. "It's so stuffy in here!" she sighed, flopping onto her bed.

Aunt Millie, who shared Kit's room, looked up from her book of Shakespeare's sonnets. "What can't be cured must be endured," she said.

Kit fanned herself with her hand. "The house feels hot and crowded to me tonight," she complained. "It's getting on my nerves."

"Anyone can get along in a palace, dear child," said Aunt Millie. "Living squashed together is a true test of character."

Kit loved Aunt Millie, but sometimes she thought it would be nice to be *alone*. She clicked on her gooseneck lamp and opened her favorite book, *Robin Hood and His Adventures*, hoping that reading would soothe and absorb her as it usually did. But the imaginary adventures of Robin Hood and his merry men didn't interest her tonight. Instead, Kit found herself staring at the photo of Charlie and his CCC buddies, which she'd propped up in front of her lamp. Kit's thoughts flew far and wide, out into the velvety black night, to Montana where Charlie was, and to the faraway places Will had been. What she longed for was a *real* adventure of her own.

❉

The next day, Kit was hanging sheets on the clothesline. A hot, sultry wind lifted the sheets so that they fluttered like moist white wings around her. Aunt Millie had set up an open-air barbershop next to the clothesline. She'd cut Stirling's hair and now she was at work on Will.

"I appreciate this, ma'am," he said. "I don't meet barbers in the jungle."

"What's the jungle?" asked Stirling.

"That's what we hoboes call our camps," explained Will. "A jungle is usually close to the railroad tracks. There's one here in Cincinnati near Union Station, right next to the river."

"Do you cook over a campfire?" asked Kit dreamily. "And tell stories about the places you've been? And sing songs, and sleep out under the stars?"

"Well . . ." Will began as if he were starting a long explanation. Then he seemed to change his mind. He answered simply, "Yep."

"I've seen some of those camps," Aunt Millie said, snipping through Will's thick hair with her sharp scissors. "They look mighty uncomfortable! Hot in summer, cold in winter, wet in the rain, and buggy to boot."

"Maybe," said Kit. "But there'd be no rugs to beat or gutters to clean. And you could just come and go as you pleased. It sounds fine to me."

Aunt Millie shook her head. "A wanderer's life is lonely and hard," she said. "I believe most people are good-hearted, but not everyone's kind to hoboes." She untied the cloth she'd put around Will's shoulders and shook the hair off it. "You're done, just plain Will," she said. "And much improved, if I do say so myself."

"Thank you, ma'am," said Will as Aunt Millie went inside. Will stood and brushed off his pants. "I sure am glad I stopped here," he said to Kit and Stirling.

"Why *did* you stop at our house?" asked Kit.

"How'd you know we'd be nice?"

"I saw the sign," said Will.

"What sign?" asked Kit and Stirling together.

"Come on," Will said, tilting his head toward the fence. "I'll show you."

Kit and Stirling followed Will to the corner of the yard where the fence met the street.

"Look," said Will. On the fencepost, someone had drawn a sketch of a cat. "That sign means a kindhearted woman lives here."

"Oh!" exclaimed Kit, enchanted. "Are there other signs, too?"

"Yep," said Will. "Lots of 'em. They're a secret code that we hoboes use to tell one another what to expect in the places we go. Usually, the sign is scratched on a fence or drawn on a building or a sidewalk with chalk or coal."

"Can you show us more?" asked Kit.

"Sure," said Will. Stirling, who liked to draw, always had a pencil stub and a piece of scrap paper in his pocket. He gave the pencil and paper to Will now.

Will drew one horizontal line. "One line means it's a doubtful place, better not stop there," he said. He added three more lines and explained, "But four lines means that the lady of the house will give you food if you do chores." Will drew a circle with two arrows pointing out of it. "This means 'get out fast,' and this . . ." he drew a big V, "means 'pretend to be sick.'"

"Why would you do that?" asked Stirling.

"If you pretend to be sick, folks will help you and feed you," said Will.

"But isn't it lying to fake an illness?" asked Kit.

"I suppose it is," said Will. "But on the road . . . well, sometimes you have to do whatever it takes to survive."

"Do you ever . . . steal?" asked Kit.

Will took a deep breath. "Let me ask you this," he said. "Say you work hard all morning helping a farmer harvest potatoes, and at the end, he gives you two wormy ones for your labor. If you slip two more potatoes in your pockets without telling him, is it stealing?"

Kit and Stirling didn't answer.

"Hunger changes the rules somewhat," said Will. He drew a circle and a square and put a dot in the middle of each. "This is the sign you'd leave on the stingy farmer's fencepost. It means a bad-tempered man lives there."

Kit nudged Stirling. "I bet *that* sign is outside Uncle Hendrick's house," she said. Kit's uncle lived downtown. He was well-to-do, very stingy, and often mean.

"Signs aren't the only way hoboes help one another," said Will. "When hoboes ride into town on the train, we go to the jungle. Then we spread out and look for chores to do for food. Maybe I sweep out a store and the storekeeper gives me a couple of onions. I bring them back to the jungle and put them together with everyone else's food to make a hobo stew. See, onions alone aren't so great. But add 'em to a pot of stew and there's more food for all, and it tastes better, too."

"Hobo stew," said Kit, savoring the words. "I wish I could try some."

❈

Will said his thank-yous and good-byes early that afternoon, explaining that he planned to spend the night in the jungle near Union Station and then hop a freight headed west the next day. Kit was very sorry to see him go.

"It's duller than ever around here," she griped to Stirling later as they took the dry sheets off the clothesline and put them in the laundry basket. "Will's the only interesting thing that's happened to us all summer."

Stirling agreed. "I liked hearing about the jungle and the hoboes," he said. He patted his pocket where he kept his pencil stub and scrap paper. "I liked the secret signs Will taught us, too."

"Didn't that hobo stew sound good?" asked Kit. All at once, she gasped. "Oh, no!" she exclaimed. "We didn't give Will anything for the stew!"

Kit and Stirling looked at each other in dismay. Then Kit had an idea. "You know what?" she said eagerly. "I bet if we asked, Mother and Aunt Millie would give us some food. We could take it down to the jungle near Union Station and give it to Will to put in the hobo stew."

"I don't—" Stirling began doubtfully.

"Listen, Stirling," Kit interrupted. "Remember that stingy farmer with the wormy potatoes Will told us about?"

Stirling nodded.

"Well, we're worse than that farmer if we don't give Will some of the tomatoes and beans he picked," said

Kit. "We owe Will some food for the stew. He worked hard helping us, didn't he?"

Stirling nodded again.

"Besides, aren't you dying to see the jungle?" said Kit. "I am!" She hoisted the laundry basket onto her hip and spoke with a mixture of determination and excitement. "As soon as I finish my chores, I'll talk to the grownups. And then we'll go find Will."

The Hobo Jungle

CHAPTER 7

No, Grace," Kit said. "You can't come with us to the jungle. Stay."

Grace sighed. She sank down, her ears puddling around her head and her droopy eyes looking sad. Kit was sorry, but Grace didn't move very fast on her short legs and her splayed feet that pointed out like a duck's. And Kit was in a hurry. She and Stirling were just setting forth and it was already late afternoon. Finishing her chores had taken longer than Kit had expected.

Talking to the grownups had, too. Mrs. Howard had said that the jungle was dangerous, probably full of thugs and murderers! But luckily, Aunt Millie had persuaded her that most hoboes were just folks who were down on their luck, and that going to the jungle would be a generous, educational thing for Kit and

Stirling to do. Mrs. Howard fussed, but she gave in after Stirling promised not to eat any of the hobo stew. Otherwise, she was sure he'd come down with some dreadful disease.

Now, finally, Kit and Stirling were on their way with a flour-sack bag full of food that Aunt Millie had packed. There were fresh tomatoes and beans from the garden, a can of stewed tomatoes, and a can of milk. Kit's stomach was fluttery. She was an honest girl, and she admitted to herself that she wanted to take food to the hoboes not just out of kindness, but also out of curiosity. The part of her that was a writer was always intrigued by new experiences. At last, she'd have something interesting to write about in her newspaper for Charlie. She'd notice everything about the jungle. And no matter what Mrs. Howard said, *she'd* taste the hobo stew!

It was not a long walk to Union Station from the Kittredges' house. Very shortly, Kit and Stirling passed the huge front of the train station. They continued past the rail yards to the riverbank underneath the trestle bridge. There, almost hidden in a little grove of trees and low bushes, was a cleared-out space of bare ground with a smoky fire in the middle of it.

"We're here," breathed Kit to Stirling. "This is the jungle."

Kit and Stirling looked around with wide eyes. Somehow, the jungle was not as comfortable-looking as Kit had imagined. There were a few tumbledown shelters made of old boards leaning against trees and a few dirty tents that sagged tiredly. The people looked tired, too. Some were washing their clothes in the river and then spreading them on bushes to dry. One man was shaving, standing at a cracked mirror hung from a tree branch. But most of the hoboes were stretched out on the ground, hard asleep, their hats covering their faces. Someone was playing a soft, haunting tune on a harmonica. The air smelled of wood smoke, coffee, and stew.

Kit was glad to see Will coming toward her.

"Hey," said Will. "Kit and Stirling, what are you doing here?"

Kit took the food out of the sack. "We came to give you this food for the hobo stew," she said. "Sorry we forgot before."

Will grinned. "Well, thanks," he said.

Will used a sharp rock to open the cans. He lifted the lid from the pot, added the canned tomatoes and the fresh tomatoes and beans from the garden, stirred the stew, and gave Kit a taste. It was very spicy. In a moment, a woman came to the fire and filled three bowls from the pot. Kit was sadly surprised when she saw that the woman was taking the stew to three very small, very hungry-looking children. One of the children was practically a baby. Will gave the young mother the can of milk.

Then he looked at Kit's face. "What's the matter?" he asked.

Kit said slowly, "I didn't expect to see little kids here." Kit had assumed that hoboes were people like Will who'd *chosen* to live an adventurous life on the road. Now she understood that most of them were poor, lost people—families with tiny babies, even— who had once been settled and respectable but now, because of the Depression, had no place to call home.

Kit saw that the young mother's husband was asleep. He'd tied his shoes to his wrist. "Why'd he do that?" Kit asked Will quietly.

"He's afraid someone will steal his shoes while he's

asleep," explained Will. "A hobo's shoes are his most valuable possession. Can't get anywhere without 'em. Men gamble for shoes, and fight for 'em, too."

Kit looked around at the other hoboes. They were wearing street shoes, tennis shoes, old rubber boots, shoes with pieces of tire nailed to the bottom, mismatched hiking boots, even rags wrapped around their feet and legs and tied on with rope. One boy had taken off a huge old pair of four-buckle galoshes. He wore two pairs of socks, and he was stuffing crumpled newspaper into the toes of the galoshes to make them fit. Another man was repairing his boots, which were clearly too small for him. When Kit saw his feet, she was heartsick and a little ashamed of herself. The way her sandals pinched her toes was nothing compared to the way this man's poor feet were rubbed raw and bleeding.

Kit's attention was suddenly distracted by a noisy group of men arriving in the jungle. They greeted the others and squatted down by the fire.

"A freight train must've pulled in," Will explained to Kit and Stirling.

One of the younger men looked up. "Well, if it isn't Texas Will," he said, smirking. He pronounced Will "whee-yull," making fun of Will's accent.

"Hello, Lex," said Will. Kit could tell that Will did not like Lex.

"Who's this?" Lex asked, pointing at Kit and Stirling.

"They're friends of mine," said Will. "They live just north of here."

"So, kids," Lex drawled, "I bet Will has told you all about me, his old friend Lex, and how I'm the world's best at hopping freights."

Kit and Stirling shook their heads no.

"He didn't?" said Lex, pretending to be surprised. "Well, come on then. I'll show you how good I am." Lex stood up. "Better yet, I'll teach you how to hop a freight. What do you say?"

"Leave 'em alone, Lex," said Will.

But Lex ignored Will and spoke straight to Kit. "There's nothing to it," he said. "The train I just got off is heading north. We'll hop it and get off at the first stop, still within the city limits. It'll be a ride toward home for you and your little buddy there." He tilted his head toward Stirling.

Everyone was quiet, waiting to see what Kit would do. She knew Lex was a braggart and not to be trusted.

But a chance to hop a freight was a chance for a *real* adventure.

"Lex is all talk, Kit," said Will. "Don't let him bamboozle you."

Lex still spoke to Kit. "I'm not talking you into anything, am I, missie?" he said in a wheedling voice. "You'd like to try it. I can tell by the look in your eyes that you're curious. Oh, but maybe you're afraid. Is that it? You scared?"

"I am not!" said Kit hotly. "I want to do it."

"No, Kit," said Will. "Hopping freights is dangerous. It's against the—"

But Kit was not listening. "*You* hop freights all the time," she cut in. "And you told me that lots of girls my age do it, too. How dangerous can it be?" Kit lowered her voice and spoke earnestly. "Don't you see, Will?" she asked. "This is my one chance to do something exciting. I *can't* let it go by." She turned to Stirling. "Listen," she said, "you don't have to come."

Stirling looked at Kit with his huge, pure gray eyes. "Yes, I do," he said.

"Let's go, then," said Lex impatiently. "The train will be leaving soon."

"This is a bad idea, Kit," said Will, frowning. "But if you're so set on it, I'm coming, too. I've got to be sure you get home safely."

Kit, Stirling, and a reluctant Will followed Lex along the riverbank, under the trestle bridge, and up a hill. They skirted the edge of the rail yard, making their way between huge freight cars and over a tangle of rails. Kit was soon so twisted around that she had no idea what direction she was headed in. At last, Lex stopped. He pointed to a red boxcar whose door was open. It was part of a train that was so long that Kit couldn't see the engine or the caboose.

"We'll jump into that boxcar," Lex said. "But we have to wait until the train moves out of the rail yard before we do."

Kit's heart beat fast with excitement while they waited for the train to move. Finally, with a slow hiss of steam, the train's wheels began to turn and the train chugged toward them, gathering speed. Lex ran along next to it with Kit, Stirling, and Will following him. Then Lex grabbed onto a metal ladder attached to the boxcar and, in a move as smooth as a cat's, swung himself up and into the open door. He made it look easy.

Kit and Stirling ran next to each other, staying even with the train. Then Stirling tripped. He started to fall forward, and for one sickening second Kit was afraid he'd be crushed under the wheels of the train. But Will caught him from behind, grabbed him by the scruff of the neck and the seat of his pants, and tossed him headfirst onto the train as if he were a sack of potatoes. Then Will swung himself up into the car, too.

The train was moving faster and faster. Kit was a good runner, but she had to run with all her might to keep up with the red boxcar. Will knelt down in the open door of the boxcar and reached out his hand to Kit.

"Grab my hand," he shouted over the noise of the train.

Kit put on a burst of speed. She stretched her arm out, reaching, reaching, *reaching* for Will's hand. At last, she caught it. Will lifted her up so that she dangled, then swung her so she flew through the air into the boxcar. Kit thudded against the hard wooden floor as she landed.

"Are you okay?" Will asked her.

Kit was too out of breath to talk, so she just nodded. Eagerly, she scrambled to her feet and stood by the open door. The wind blew her hair every which way, smoke stung her eyes, and cinders smudged her face, but she didn't care. Faster and faster the train rushed along the track, until the world outside was just a blur. Kit was exhilarated. She'd never moved so fast! She'd never felt so free! For a second, for a heartbeat, Kit wished the train would never stop.

Then Stirling tugged on her arm. "Kit!" he said urgently. "Lex led us to the wrong train. We're not going north, toward home. We're going south, across the river. Look!"

Kit stuck her head out. Sure enough, the train was barreling across the trestle bridge, the tracks spooling out behind it, the river flowing below. With every click of the wheels, Cincinnati grew smaller and home was farther away.

Kit whirled around. "Lex!" she shouted, searching for his face in the dimness of the boxcar. "Did you trick us on purpose?"

Lex didn't answer. Because just then, the brakes slammed on and the train *screeched* to a stop. Kit held on tight to the door to keep from falling. She looked out to see where they were. The train had crossed the bridge. It was stopped in a wooded area where a dirt road crossed the railroad tracks. Kit saw lots of men coming toward the train.

"This is trouble!" muttered Lex. He knocked Kit out of his way, leaped out of the boxcar, and disappeared into the trees.

Will held a finger to his lips and gestured for Kit and Stirling to stand up and press themselves against the wall behind him. Outside, Kit heard angry voices and the sound of fists and sticks pounding on the boxcars.

"Will!" Kit whispered. "What's happening?"

"The train's been stopped by railroad bulls," answered Will. "Bulls are men the railroad hires to throw hoboes off the trains." He pulled off his cap. "Put this on," he said to Kit. "I don't want them to know you're a girl."

"Why?" Kit started to ask. But suddenly, she was blinded by a flashlight aimed straight into her eyes. Will and Stirling froze in the light, too.

"All right!" growled a harsh voice. "Are you bums going to come out by yourselves, or do I have to come in there and toss you out like trash?"

"Come on!" ordered another voice. "Out!"

Will jumped out of the boxcar. He turned to help Kit and Stirling, but one of the railroad bulls shoved him aside, grasped the two smaller children each by an arm, and jerked them out so roughly that they fell onto the dusty, rocky ground. Kit stood. She tried to brush the dirt off her overalls, but it just smeared. She wiped her hands on the seat of her pants.

Outside the boxcar was a scene of scary confusion. Railroad bulls swarmed over the train, hauling hoboes out of the boxcars, shouting, and pushing the hoboes into a double line. The railroad bulls carried stout sticks and bats. Some even had guns. Stirling stood right next to Kit, and Will stood in front of them, trying to shield them as best he could from the bulls.

But it was no use. One of the bulls rapped Kit sharply on the back of her legs with his club. "Line up, you bum!" the bull ordered.

Kit spoke fiercely. "I'm not a bum," she said.

"Hah!" scoffed the man. He eyed Kit's filthy overalls, dirty hands, and sooty face. "You look like a bum to me. Get in line. Be quick about it." He pushed Kit into line between Stirling and Will.

"Where are they taking us?" Kit asked Will as they walked forward.

"To town," said Will. "Keep my cap on your head. Hide your hair. If they see that you're a girl, they'll separate us at the jail."

"Jail?" gasped Kit. "Why are we going to jail? We didn't do anything wrong. We're not criminals!"

"Hopping a freight is against the law," said Will. "I tried to tell you, but you wouldn't listen. And they put us in jail so that we won't beg or panhandle in their town. We'll spend the night in a cell. In the morning, they'll put us in a truck and drive us out of town."

Spend the night in jail? thought Kit miserably. She looked behind her to see if there was any way to escape. But the double line of hoboes, about twenty in all, was closely guarded by bulls on all sides. The pitiful parade left the woods and entered a town called Spencerville. As the hoboes passed, the townspeople stared and frowned at them with dislike and distrust.

The jail was a squat brick building that faced the town square. Its walls were thick, and its front windows had bars. Kit and the others were herded inside. "Turn your pockets inside out," the sheriff ordered them.

Kit and Will had empty pockets, and the sheriff let Stirling keep his scrap of paper and pencil stub. Then all the hoboes were crowded into a small, square room. It had a concrete floor and one tiny window, but no furniture. The hoboes filed in silently and sat on the hard floor or slouched tiredly against the walls. Kit stood close to Will and Stirling. The wall was cold against her back. Tears pricked her eyes as she watched the door swing shut and heard it lock with a hollow, horrifying *clang*.

Do Something

it shivered.

"Don't be afraid," said Will softly.

"I'm not," said Kit, though she was. "I'm mad. We've got to get out of here. We've got to *do* something."

Stirling gave her an earnest look, but he said nothing.

Soon, there was a loud rattle and clatter in the hall. The door opened and the sheriff announced, "Dinner." All the hoboes stood and formed a line.

They were each given a mug of water and a tin plate with a cold boiled potato, a spoonful of beans, and a slice of soggy, moldy bread on it. Though Kit was hungry, she had to force herself to eat. The food smelled sour. It stuck in her throat so that she had to wash it down with the rusty-tasting water.

After dinner, the sheriff brought wash basins of
cold water, bars of hard soap, and newspapers for
towels for the hoboes to use to wash up. Kit gathered
her courage and went to the sheriff.

"Please, sir," she said. "There's been a mistake. My
friends and I aren't hoboes. My parents don't have a
phone, but please let me call my Uncle Hendrick back
in Cincinnati. He'll tell my parents and they'll come
get us."

The sheriff crossed his arms over his chest. "If you
have relatives in Cincinnati," he said, "what were you
doing on the train? You bums! Always making up
stories, like you've got an uncle who'll help you." He
shook his head. "You think I believe that lie?"

"Please let me phone," said Kit. "You'll see I'm telling the truth."

"Hmph!" the sheriff snorted. "Where's your money
for the call?"

"Well," said Kit. "I don't have any money. But—"

"Of course you don't," interrupted the sheriff. He
laughed a mean laugh. "Nice try, boy. You're a good
panhandler. But I've seen too many of you beggars
to fall for your tricks. Where would I be if I let every

tramp who asked me make a free phone call? In the
poorhouse, that's where."

Kit stamped her foot. "I'm not a beggar!" she said.

"That's enough, boy!" said the sheriff. "Don't you
get sassy! And take your hat off when you're speaking
to me." Before Kit could stop him, he snatched Will's
cap off her head. "Look at you," he snarled as he tossed
the cap at her. "A girl! I *knew* you were a liar. Come
with me. I'm going to put you in a separate cell."

"No!" said Kit furiously. She did not want to be
separated from Will and Stirling. She struggled against
the sheriff, but he was too strong for her. He held her
tightly by the arm and pulled her along behind him.

Just before she passed through the door, Stirling
yanked hard on her sleeve. Kit looked at him. He
held up his scrap of paper, and on it, Kit saw that he'd
drawn a sign shaped like a V.

Kit knew it was one of the hobo signs. *But which
one?* she thought frantically. *What does it mean?* Suddenly, she remembered.

Kit bent forward and grabbed her stomach with
her free hand. "Ohhh," she groaned. She tugged on the
sheriff's arm and slumped against the wall. "Ohhh, my

stomach. Please, sir, I feel sick." It wasn't a lie. The dinner *was* churning in her queasy stomach. Kit groaned again and held her hand over her mouth. "Please, let me go to the bathroom!"

"Oh, all right!" barked the sheriff, exasperated. He pointed. "In there."

Kit skittered into the bathroom. The second the door closed behind her, she looked around wildly, thinking, *Is there a way out? Oh, there has to be!* Then, high up the wall, she saw a little window. It was much too small for a grown person to fit through, but—

Bang, bang! The sheriff hammered on the door, growling, "Hurry up!"

"Yes, sir," Kit answered. Silently, carefully, she climbed up on the sink and opened the window. She poked her head and shoulders out, hoisted herself up, and slithered through, landing hard on the ground below. Kit scrambled to her feet. She leaned against the wall of the jail and allowed herself one shaky breath. Then she took off running. There was not a moment to lose. The sheriff would soon realize that she was gone.

Oh, please don't let anyone see me, she prayed as she ran.

But Kit had gone only a few yards when she heard,

"Hey, you! Stop!" She looked over her shoulder. Men outside the jail had spotted her and were chasing after her, shouting, "Come back, you!" Kit ran as fast as she could, trying desperately to get away from the footsteps she could hear close behind her. A rough hand grabbed her shoulder. "Gotcha!" a man panted.

"No!" shrieked Kit. She wrenched her shoulder out of his grasp. The man lost his balance and fell behind her with a heavy thud. This time Kit didn't look back. She ran for all she was worth, pelting down the dirt road out of Spencerville, toward the railroad tracks. *Home,* she thought. *I've got to get home and get help for Stirling and Will!*

On and on Kit ran. Finally, up ahead, she saw the railroad tracks, shining silver, sharp as lightning in the darkness. She trotted next to them a short distance. Then she stopped dead. *Oh, no,* she thought. Below her was the river and looming above her was the railroad trestle bridge. It wasn't a solid bridge with a road on it. Instead, it was made of crisscrossed metal girders that looked like the strands of a gigantic spiderweb spun across the river. The train tracks that crossed the bridge were supported by wooden railroad ties with big gaps between them. *How will I ever cross this bridge?* Kit worried. *Jump from tie to tie? Balance on a rail as if it were a tightrope? If only there were another way to cross the river! If only there were another way home!*

But Kit had no choice. Slowly, she walked toward the bridge. She saw that there was a narrow catwalk, two boards wide, that ran alongside the train tracks. Kit took a deep breath. Gingerly, she put one foot on the catwalk to see if it would hold her weight. It did, so she eased her other foot onto it, too. The catwalk boards were spattered with oil, which made them slippery. Kit stood up straight, holding her arms out for balance. She tried not to look down. She tried not to hear the rushing river below. She knew that if she slipped, she might fall between the girders, and the river would sweep her away. Very cautiously, she slid one foot forward, then the other. *I can do it,* she said to herself. *I can cross this bridge. I* **have** *to.*

Clouds covered the moon, making it so Kit couldn't see far ahead. The bridge seemed to disappear into nothingness. All Kit could do was put one foot slowly, carefully, fearfully in front of the other and walk forward. The boards of the catwalk were uneven, and Kit

stubbed her toe and stumbled, almost falling. *Just walk,*
she urged herself. *Keep going.* Step by scary step, Kit
inched her way along the catwalk until she was in the
middle of the bridge. *I'm halfway across now,* she realized. *There's no turning back.*

Suddenly, the boards began to tremble under her
feet. An eerie, mournful whistle pierced the air. It
seemed to cut right through Kit.

"Oh, no!" she shrieked. A train was coming straight
toward her and there was nowhere to go.

I'm trapped! thought Kit. Desperately, Kit did the
only thing she could. She flung herself down on her
stomach and stretched herself flat against the catwalk.
She held onto the boards with both hands, pressed her
face into the splintery, oily wood, and closed her eyes.
With a howling *whoosh!* the train pushed the air in
front of it. With a monstrous force, it shook the bridge
violently. With a deafening roar, it thundered past,
just a few feet from Kit. She could feel its hot, fiery
breath on her back. Beneath her, the boards rattled
and bounced, as if trying to toss her off into the water
below. Kit held on for dear life.

Then, as suddenly as it had appeared, the train was

gone, screaming off into the dark. For a moment, Kit
couldn't move. Then she spoke to herself sternly. *Get
up. Get up and go.* Slowly, she lifted her face. Her fingers
had gripped the boards so tightly that they ached when
she let go. She pushed herself to her knees and, shakily,
she stood. On wobbly legs, she made herself take one
step forward, then another, and another. *I've got to get
home,* she told herself over and over again. *I've got to get
help for Stirling and Will.*

The bridge and the darkness seemed endless. But
after a long, weary time, Kit blinked. *Are those lights?*
she wondered, squinting at pinpoints that danced
ahead of her. *It's the city!* she realized. Kit longed to
quicken her steps, but she knew that would be dangerous. She had to hold herself back, force herself to walk
slowly and carefully, until at last her feet were on solid
ground and the bridge was behind her. Kit was so
relieved that she wanted to collapse, but she couldn't
allow herself to stop. She pushed on, past the rail yards,
past Union Station, and through the city streets. The
short, easy route she and Stirling had traveled on their
way to the hoboes' jungle earlier that day felt long and
difficult going the other way now. Kit was so footsore

and tired that it took all of her strength to put one foot in front of the other.

As she trudged up the last hill to home, Kit's heart dragged as much as her feet. *Why did I hop that freight?* she thought. *How could I have been so stupid?* Desperate as she was to get home, Kit dreaded facing Mother, Dad, Aunt Millie, and Stirling's mother. *They'll be so angry!* she thought.

When at last Kit saw her house ahead of her, she broke into a run, and hot tears spilled out of her eyes. "Dad! Mother!" she called out, wiping the tears from her cheeks.

The front door opened and yellow light poured out across the lawn. Dad, Mother, Aunt Millie, and Mrs. Howard rushed outside together, and Dad ran forward to catch Kit in his arms.

"Where have you been?" he asked. "Are you all right? Mr. Peck went down to the jungle to find you. We've been frantic! What's happened?"

"Where's Stirling?" asked Mrs. Howard.

For a moment, Kit didn't try to answer. She buried her face in Dad's chest and held on tight. She knew that all her whole life long she would never forget this

feeling, this wonderful feeling of being home and safe at
last. Then she pulled away from Dad. "I'm so sorry. It's
all my fault!" she sputtered. "I wanted an adventure,
and I didn't stop to think . . ." She stopped, and swallowed hard. "Will and Stirling are across the river," she
said, "in Spencerville. They're . . . they're in jail."

"What?" gasped all the grownups, bewildered. Mrs.
Howard held on to Mother as if she were going to faint.

As swiftly as she could, Kit told the whole story.
She told how she'd been so stubbornly set on having an
adventure that she'd hopped the freight even though
Will tried to talk her out of it. She described being
rounded up by the railroad bulls and marched to jail.
She told how Stirling scribbled the secret sign, and how
she escaped, crossed the trestle bridge, and made her
way home. Then she turned her dirt- and tear-streaked
face to Dad. "We've got to go to Spencerville and rescue
Will and Stirling *right now*," she pleaded. "We've got to
get them out of that jail."

Dad nodded. "We'll take Mr. and Mrs. Bell's car," he
said. "Come on."

❅

When they got out of the car in Spencerville and walked into the jail, Kit held tightly to Dad's hand. She stood very close, hidden behind him, while he talked to the sheriff about letting Will and Stirling go.

"Go ahead and take these boys," the sheriff said as he released Will and Stirling. "We don't like their sort around here."

Will and Stirling hurried toward Dad with grateful expressions. All three turned toward the door. But Kit held back. She stepped fully into the light so that the sheriff could see her clearly.

"You!" exclaimed the sheriff. "You should be ashamed of yourself!"

Kit looked the sheriff straight in the eyes and spoke in a level voice. "Sir," she said, "I think *you* should be ashamed."

"Hopping freight trains is against the law," said the sheriff. "It's my job to keep bums off trains."

"You don't have to be so mean about it," said Kit. "The hoboes haven't hurt anybody. They're just poor. There's no reason to treat them so badly. It isn't right. And it isn't *fair*."

The sheriff glowered, but he said nothing.

"Come along, Kit," said Dad softly. "It's time to go home."

Kit followed Stirling, Will, and Dad to the car. Stirling climbed into the backseat and Kit sat next to him, leaving room for Will to sit in the front. But Will didn't get into the car.

Kit poked her head out. "Aren't you coming, Will?" she asked.

Will shook his head. "No," he said. "Thanks, but it's time for me to head west to Oregon. I don't want to miss getting a job during the apple harvest."

"Is Montana on your way?" asked Kit.

"I reckon so," said Will. "I'll stop by and say 'hey' to Charlie for you."

Will shook Dad's hand. "Good-bye, sir," he said. "Thanks for everything." Then he smiled his wide, heartwarming grin at Kit and Stirling. "Good-bye, you two," he said.

This time Kit and Stirling could not smile back. "Good-bye, Will," they said. Stirling's voice was low in the darkness, and Kit's voice was sorrowful. She was weighted down with worry, now that she knew how hard Will's life really was. Dad started the car, and

Kit knelt on the seat and looked out the back window to wave good-bye to Will. But he had already turned away. He was walking west.

❧

Scrubbed clean, and in their bathrobes, Kit and Stirling sat at the kitchen table. As soon as they'd arrived home, Mother had told them to take baths, then report to the kitchen. Now an unsmiling Aunt Millie poured them tall glasses of cold milk and put plates of hot, buttered toast in front of them.

Mother spoke first. "We are very glad you're safe, children," she said.

"We were worried sick about you!" exclaimed Mrs. Howard.

"We're sorry," said Kit. "We—"

But Dad held up his hand to stop her. "I understand how it feels to want an adventure," he said. "Sometimes I think the toughest thing about this Depression is enduring it, day after day. But I hope you two understand that what you did was foolish and dangerous. You used poor judgment, and you're lucky you didn't have to pay for it more dearly than you did. I think I speak for Mrs.

Howard and Mother and Aunt Millie when I say that we're disappointed in you. We need to trust you to be more sensible in the future. Do you understand?"

Kit and Stirling nodded. They both looked ashamed.

"Well!" said Aunt Millie briskly. "Thank goodness it's all over now. And as Shakespeare says, 'All's well that ends well.'"

Kit managed a weak smile. But as she went up the stairs to her room, with Mother's gentle arm around her, Kit thought that perhaps this time Shakespeare and Aunt Millie were not right. Kit thought of Will and all the hardship that was before him. She thought of the hungry children she'd seen eating the hobo stew. She thought of the poor, tired hoboes gathered around their fire in the jungle, resting their weary, hurt feet. She thought of the hoboes crowded so roughly into the terrible jail. For them, all was not ended and, surely, all was not well.

After Mother kissed her good night, Kit lay awake thinking. *Everyone should see what I saw today,* she thought. *Hoboes have a hard life. People should know that. Someone should tell them. Someone should **do** something. Maybe I could.*

Something Wonderful

 it and her family liked hearing from Will after he went west. Every month or so, a postcard would arrive from a new place. Kit and Dad would look at the atlas to find the state Will was writing from—Oregon, California, Oklahoma. Will always scrawled a few breezy sentences on the cards, and sounded happy. But Kit knew that most of his travels were far from pleasant. She could not forget the hobo children's hungry faces, or the sad squalor of the hobo jungle. She did what she could to help; she and Ruthie and Stirling took food to the jungle several times. When winter set in—cruelly cold, dark, and harsh—Kit was even more determined to find a way to help the hobo families.

Things had changed for her own family. Charlie finished his CCC job in Montana and came home to fill the house with his great laughter and energy. And finally, after years of hoping and trying, one day Dad came home with the best news in the world. He had a job. It was only a part-time job working at the airport and it didn't pay much, but it was a real job that he could count on. Kit knew that her family still had to pinch pennies and rely on the money the boarders paid, but Mother and Dad both looked a little less worried now, and they smiled a lot more often.

Kit was feeling cheerful as she walked home from school with Ruthie and Stirling on this gray February afternoon. Kit's old coat was almost too small to button shut anymore, so she tugged it tighter against the chill as she hurried down the sidewalk toward home and bounded up the steps to her house.

Somehow, the minute Kit, Ruthie, and Stirling walked in the door, Kit knew something wonderful was about to happen.

Mother was waiting for them in the front hall. "Here you are at last," she said, sounding cheerfully impatient. "Hang up your coats. Then come join me in the living room."

Mother left, and Kit turned to Ruthie and Stirling.

"I wonder what's up," she whispered.

Ruthie shrugged and Stirling said, "Who knows?" But Kit saw them slip sly smiles to each other, so she knew they were in cahoots with Mother.

The children hurriedly hung up their coats, took off their boots, and rushed into the living room. Stirling's mother, Mrs. Howard, was there looking happy and fluttery. Charlie had a smile a mile wide. Miss Hart and Miss Finney simply beamed. Even Grace, Kit's dog, wore a goofy, drooly, doggy grin. But no one looked happier than Mother as she came toward Kit.

"This is for you, dear," Mother said. She was holding a winter coat. It was made of dark gray wool tweed flecked with blue. It had deep pockets and cuffs, four big buttons, and a belt.

"Wow," breathed Kit.

"Try it on!" said Ruthie. "See how it fits."

"Yes," insisted everyone. "Go ahead."

Kit hesitated. "It's a beautiful coat," she said. "I really like it. But . . . isn't a new coat like this awfully expensive?"

Much to Kit's surprise, everyone laughed.

"This coat isn't new," said Mother. "It belonged to Dad."

Mrs. Howard piped up. "Your mother and I took his old coat apart, washed the material, cut it to size, and made a new coat for you using the material inside out," she said proudly. "Wasn't that clever of us?"

"It sure was," agreed Kit, who believed that her mother was the cleverest mother in the world. "I like the coat even more knowing that it's not exactly new," she said. She grinned, thinking how Aunt Millie, who was back in Kentucky now, would have approved of Mother's project. This was definitely a "waste-not, want-not" kind of coat.

"Good," said Miss Hart. "Then you'll like our surprise, too." She winked at Miss Finney and Ruthie.

"Ta da!" sang Miss Finney. She and Ruthie presented Kit with a knitted red hat and blue-and-red mittens.

"These aren't exactly new, either," Ruthie said. "The red yarn came from an old sweater of Stirling's that we unraveled, and the blue yarn came from a cap of Charlie's that Grace chewed."

"Unfortunately, Grace and I have the same taste in caps," said Charlie. He crossed his arms over his chest and pretended to frown down at Grace. But Grace, far from looking ashamed, seemed pleased with herself for her part in the creation of the mittens. She thumped her tail importantly.

"Go on, Kit," said Ruthie. "We're dying to see how everything looks."

Mother held the coat as Kit slipped her arms into the sleeves. Then Kit buttoned the buttons, buckled the belt, and pulled on the mittens and the hat.

"The hat goes like this," said Mother, tilting Kit's hat *just so*. "There," she said. "Perfect. Now turn around so we can see the whole effect."

Kit spun around. Charlie whistled, Stirling clapped, and all the ladies *oohed* and *aahed*. Kit blushed. She felt a little bashful about being the center of attention. But she knew that everyone was glad to have an excuse to make a happy fuss. Back before the Depression began, when her family had plenty of money, no one would have carried on much about a new coat. Now it was something to celebrate.

"Oh, look!" said Mrs. Howard. "Everything fits like a dream."

"And it's so stylish!" added Miss Finney.

"The coat makes you look really tall, Kit," said Ruthie with an approving air. "The whole outfit is very grown-up."

"I love it," Kit said. "Thank you, every one of you. It's wonderful. All of it." Kit held the collar to her nose and took a deep, delicious breath of the clean-smelling, woolly material. She felt warm and cozy, all the more so because the coat and hat and mittens had been made for her by her friends and family out of things that had belonged to them. It was as if affection had been sewn into the seams of the stout wool coat and knitted into the hat and mittens to cover Kit with warmth from head to toe. She sighed a sigh of pure pleasure. "It was very nice of all of you to make these things for me," she said.

"Well, you desperately needed a new coat," said Mother. "Your old coat has been too small for two years now."

Kit had a sudden thought. "Mother," she asked, "do we need my old coat? Are you planning to take it apart and make something out of *it*, too?"

"Why, no," answered Mother. "I don't think so."

"Then may I give it away?" asked Kit. She ex-

plained, "I keep thinking about the children Stirling
and I saw in the hobo jungle last summer. This cold
weather must be terrible for them." Kit remembered
the children's worn-out shoes and their thin, ragged
clothes. "Would it be all right if Stirling and Ruthie and
I went to the hobo jungle this afternoon?" she asked
Mother. "Maybe there's a girl there who could use my
old coat."

"I think that's a very good idea," said Mother. She
turned to Mrs. Howard and asked, "Is it all right with
you if Stirling goes, too?"

Mrs. Howard nodded. "As long as they stay away
from the trains," she said, "and come home before
dark."

"We'll be back in time to do our chores before dinner," Kit promised.

"Hurry along, then," said Mother. "And Ruthie, be
sure to stop by your house and ask your mother for
permission to go."

"I will!" said Ruthie.

Kit folded her old coat over her arm as Ruthie and
Stirling put their coats and boots back on. Then the
children went outside, bundled up against the February

afternoon. Kit smiled. She hardly felt the cold, snug as she was in her not-exactly-new, wonderful winter coat, hat, and mittens!

❋

Ruthie's mother gave Ruthie permission to go. She also gave the children a sack of potatoes for the hoboes. The children took turns carrying the sack as they walked through town and past the front of Union Station. Kit was sure of the way. But when they came to the spot next to the river where the hobo jungle had been during the summer, it was deserted.

"Where'd the jungle go?" asked Stirling.

"Are you sure we're in the right place?" asked Ruthie.

Kit looked around. Not one tired hobo was lying asleep on the ground with his hat over his face, or resting his weary feet, or repairing his travel-worn shoes. There were no tents or rickety lean-tos propped against the trees, no hungry children eating stew, no clothes spread on the bushes to dry as there'd been in the summer. There was no fire inside the circle of stones on the windswept, bare ground, no scent of coffee, no music. All was oddly quiet.

"Hey," said Stirling. "Look."

He pointed, and Kit and Ruthie saw smoke rising up, dark gray like a pencil squiggle against the pale winter sky. The smoke was coming straight out of the ground! Kit looked more closely and saw that someone had dug a cavelike shelter into the embankment under the bridge. There was even a door built into the hillside.

"Come on," Kit said. She knocked on the door.

A man with a weather-beaten face opened it. "Yes?" he asked. His gruff voice reminded Kit of stern Uncle Hendrick.

"Excuse me, sir," Kit said politely. "But where are all the hoboes?"

"Someplace south, if they're smart," said the man. "There are five of us living in this cave and we don't have room for any more."

"But what about the ones who are riding the rails?" asked Kit. "Lots of people camped here last summer when they were passing through town."

"Humph!" harrumphed the man. "Don't you know that this is Cincinnati's coldest winter in twenty-nine years? Folks'd freeze to death camping out. Most hoboes who are passing through go to soup kitchens or missions. Sometimes they can stay for a night or two if they do chores. Then they have to move on."

"Oh, I see," said Kit. She thanked the man, and Ruthie gave him the sack of potatoes. Then Kit, Stirling, and Ruthie walked to the soup kitchen on River Street. They'd once delivered a Thanksgiving basket of food there, so they knew to go to the back door to make their delivery. They went inside and carefully made their way past the stoves steaming with pots of soup, around the busy people making sandwiches and coffee, and through the swinging door to the front part of the soup kitchen where the food was served.

The three children stopped still and stared at the crowded room. An endless line of men, women, and children shuffled in the front door and past the tables where soup, bread, and coffee were served. Every seat at every table was taken, so many people had to eat standing up. Groups of people, grim and gray, were gathered in the corners. Families huddled together wherever they could and spoke in low murmurs. Somewhere a baby was crying. *So many people,* thought Kit sadly, *young and old, and all so hungry and poor.*

Kit knew that only luck and chance separated her

family from those she saw around her. Almost two
years ago her own father had come to this very soup
kitchen to get food for her family because he had run
out of money. That year they fell so far behind in pay-
ing the mortgage that they would have been evicted—
thrown out of their house—if Aunt Millie had not
rescued them with her life savings. Things were better
for Kit's family now. But the Depression had taught Kit
that nothing was certain. Everything could change suddenly, and she could find herself standing in line for
soup, just like these children.

It made Kit's heart hurt to see them. One child was
wearing a filthy, worn-out, threadbare coat that was
much too small. Another wore a ragged overcoat that
dragged on the ground. One even wore a blanket tied
around his waist with rope. Their shoes were even
worse. Some of the children had nothing but rags
wrapped around their feet. Others wore broken-down
boots with no laces, rubber galoshes they'd lined with
old newspapers, or too-small shoes with the front part
cut so that their toes poked out.

Ruthie tugged on Kit's sleeve. She nodded her head
toward an area where people were sitting on the floor,

leaning against the wall. "There's someone who needs your coat," she said.

At first, all Kit could see was what looked like a pile of dirty rags. But then she saw a little girl's thin, pinched face above the rags, and she realized that the rags were the little girl's skimpy coat—or what was left of it. It was badly stained and torn. The pockets had been ripped off and used to patch the elbows, and all the buttons but one were gone. The little girl was cuddled up to her mother. Her hair was tangled, her eyes were dull, and she seemed as lifeless and colorless as a shadow.

Kit, Ruthie, and Stirling went over and quietly stood in front of the girl and her mother. Kit held out her old coat. "Ma'am," she said to the mother, "may I give this coat to your little girl?"

The woman didn't answer. She looked at Kit as if she didn't quite believe what she had heard. But the little girl stood up. Shyly, eagerly, she took the coat from Kit and put it on over her ragged one. She smoothed the front of the coat with both hands, and then she raised her face to Kit. In that moment, something wonderful happened. The little girl was transformed from a ghost to a real girl. She hugged herself, and her pale cheeks glowed. "Thank you," she said to Kit, smiling a smile that lit her whole face.

Kit smiled back. "You're very welcome," she said. She could tell that the little girl felt the same way *she* had felt about *her* new coat. It warmed her both inside and out.

Bright, brilliant streaks of pink and purple were splashed across the late-afternoon sky as Kit, Ruthie, and Stirling walked home from the soup kitchen.

"Kit, you were like the fairy godmother who turned Cinderella's rags into a ball gown," said Ruthie, who liked fairy tales. "You gave that girl your old coat and *whoosh.*" She waved an imaginary wand. "You changed her."

"Maybe," said Kit. "But that was just one coat and just one kid. Every kid there needed a coat—and shoes."

"Those poor kids," said Ruthie, "having to sleep on the floor! It's terrible that there's no better place for them to stay. Isn't there *anywhere* their parents could look for help?"

"I think," said Stirling, "they *are* looking for help. That's why they're on the road. Maybe they heard about jobs in New York or California. Or maybe they ran out of money and lost their homes, so they're traveling to friends or family, hoping to be taken in. They don't have any money for train fare, so they have to ride the rails. They can't pay for a hotel, so they eat and sleep at soup kitchens for a day or two. Then they're on their way again."

"In the freezing cold," added Kit. "In their ragged coats and worn-out shoes." She sighed. If only she had a hundred coats to give away, and a hundred pairs of shoes. *That* would be wonderful.

❈

Kit and Stirling said good-bye to Ruthie at the end of her driveway and arrived home just as dusk fell. Kit went straight to work doing her evening chores. As she fed the dog and the chickens, scrubbed potatoes, and set the table for dinner, she remembered the hobo in his cheerless cave and the people in the crowded soup kitchen. *How lucky I am*, she thought. Her house might not be fancy. In fact, it was getting rather shabby. But it was warm and filled with good-hearted people who cared for one another.

Dinner was jolly that night. Afterward, Mr. Peck played his bass fiddle and Charlie played the piano. They made "Music to Do the Dishes By," and everyone sang along. Mother never used to allow the boarders to help clean up, but she had relaxed a bit and treated them more like family now. Stirling and Mrs. Howard sang as they cleared the table. Miss Hart and Miss Finney chimed in as they helped Mother wash the dishes. And Dad and Kit sang in harmony as they dried. Grace, who never liked to be left out, howled.

They were making so much noise that they didn't hear Mr. Smithens, Ruthie's father, knocking on the front door. They were surprised when he stepped into the kitchen.

"Excuse me, folks," Mr. Smithens said. "I'm sorry to barge in. But we had a call for you on our telephone." The Kittredges could not afford a telephone, so the Smithenses kindly took calls for them. "It was Cincinnati Hospital," Mr. Smithens said to Mother and Dad. "It seems that your Uncle Hendrick had a fall and broke his ankle and his wrist. They've patched him up, and he's fine. But the nurse said he's making quite a ruckus. He wants you to come immediately and pick him up and bring him back here so that you can care for him until he's back on his feet. I'll drive you to the hospital as soon as you're ready to go."

"Thank you, Stan," said Dad. "We'll be right with you."

Mother had already taken off her apron and put on her hat and coat. In a minute, she and Dad were gone. The door closed behind them, and Kit stood in the sudden silence in the chilly front hall. *Oh no,* she thought, her heart sinking lower and lower as the news sank in. *Cranky, crabby, cantankerous Uncle Hendrick is coming to stay in our house. It'll be terrible.*

To Do

e've got to think of *something* to write," said Kit.

It was Saturday morning, and Kit, Ruthie, and Stirling were up in Kit's attic room, sitting around her typewriter. They were working on a newspaper. When new boarders arrived, Kit always made a special newspaper to welcome them and to introduce them to the other boarders. Usually, Kit's head was so full of things to write that her fingers couldn't move fast enough on the typewriter keys to keep up. In this case, however, the new boarders were Uncle Hendrick and his stinky dog, Inky. They'd been living with the Kittredges for more than a week, and so far, they had not endeared themselves to anyone. Even Grace, who liked *everybody* and lavished slobbery affection on complete strangers, kept her distance from Inky and showed a cool indifference to Uncle Hendrick. Kit couldn't think of anything to write about them that was both enthusiastic and honest.

"You could take a photograph of Uncle Hendrick," suggested Stirling. Kit had an old camera that her brother, Charlie, had fixed for her, and she was eager to use it. "A picture tells more about a person than words ever could."

"Maybe, but it costs money to get the film developed," said Kit, "so I was kind of hoping to take pictures of things I really liked."

"How about a drawing?" said Ruthie. "You're a good artist, Stirling. You could draw a picture of Uncle Hendrick."

"And Inky, too," added Kit.

"All right," said Stirling, opening up his sketchpad. "Under my drawing I'll write, 'His bark is worse than his bite.'"

"Whose?" asked Ruthie, looking impish. "Inky's or Uncle Hendrick's?"

Kit smiled weakly at Ruthie's joke. Personally, she thought Uncle Hendrick's biting remarks were just as bad as the orders he barked at her.

Caring for Uncle Hendrick had turned out to be Kit's job. Mother was much too busy, and Dad was often working at the airport. Charlie helped out while Kit was at school. But when she was home, Uncle Hendrick and Inky were her responsibility, and they were a big one.

Uncle Hendrick was staying in the room that Mr. and Mrs. Bell had rented until Mr. Bell got a new job a month ago. But the room was on the second floor, and Uncle Hendrick said he couldn't go up and down the stairs because of his ankle. Before school, Kit had to bring him his morning newspaper and his breakfast tray. She also had to walk Inky. Uncle Hendrick dozed all day, so when Kit came home from school, he was fully awake, full of pepper and vinegar, and full of demands and commands. He always made a big To Do list for Kit. Then he made a big speech about how to do everything on the To Do list. Then he made a big to-do about how she had done everything wrong on yesterday's To Do list.

And tasks and errands were not all. Uncle Hendrick grew bored sitting in his room with no one but Inky for company. He expected Kit to entertain him. During the first few days, Charlie had helped by playing checkers with Uncle Hendrick. But Charlie had won too often, and now Uncle Hendrick didn't want to play checkers with him anymore. He preferred badgering Kit. His idea of a conversation was to snap at her, "What's the capital of Maine?" or, "How much is seven percent of three hundred ninety-two?" Having Uncle Hendrick in the house was every bit as terrible as Kit had thought it would be.

"Let's just write in our newspaper that we're sorry Uncle Hendrick hurt his ankle and his wrist, and we hope he is better soon," said Stirling.

"That's good," said Kit. She swiveled her chair around to face the desk and began *clickety-clacking* away on her old black typewriter. "And it's true, because the sooner he's better, the sooner he and Inky can go home!"

"The headline could be, 'The Sooner, The Better!'" joked Ruthie.

Suddenly, *bang, bang, bang!* A thunderous thumping shook the floor under the children's feet. It was accompanied by ferocious barking.

"Yikes!" said Ruthie, covering her ears. "What's *that?*"

"That's Uncle Hendrick calling me," said Kit. "His room is right under the attic. He whacks his ceiling with his cane and then Inky barks." She sighed. "I'd better go see what they want."

"Go!" said Ruthie. "Stirling and I will finish up the newspaper."

"Thanks," said Kit. She gave up her chair to Ruthie, then pelted down the stairs and poked her head into Uncle Hendrick's room. "Do you need me, Uncle Hendrick?" she asked, shouting to be heard.

Uncle Hendrick stopped walloping the ceiling. Inky stopped barking, but threw in a few extra yips and growls for good measure. "What on earth was that infernal racket coming from upstairs?" asked Uncle Hendrick crossly.

Privately, Kit thought that Uncle Hendrick and Inky were the ones who'd made the racket. But she answered politely, "I was typing. Ruthie and Stirling and I are making a newspaper."

"What a waste of time," Uncle Hendrick snorted. "Making a pretend newspaper. Writing nonsense! Haven't you outgrown such silly childishness?"

Kit lifted her chin. She was rather proud of her

newspapers. She never wrote nonsense. She loved writing, respected words, and tried hard to find the perfect ones to use, which was not the least bit childish to do. Now, for example, the perfect word to describe how she felt would be *annoyed*.

But Uncle Hendrick didn't notice her annoyance. As usual, he was concerned only about what he wanted. "Sit down!" he ordered. "I'll give you something worthwhile to write. Take a letter!"

Uncle Hendrick had broken the wrist on his right hand—his writing hand—so when he wanted to send a letter, he had to dictate it to Kit. Sometimes Kit thought that Uncle Hendrick had named his dog "Inky" because ink was something he liked to use so much. Almost every day, Uncle Hendrick dictated a letter. Usually it was a letter to the editor of the newspaper. And usually it was about "that man in the White House," which was what Uncle Hendrick called President Franklin Delano Roosevelt. Uncle Hendrick did not approve of FDR, which was what most people called the president. He did not like FDR's wife, Eleanor, either. As far as he was concerned, everything that was wrong with the country was their fault. Today Uncle

Hendrick's angry letter was in response to a newspaper article he'd read about the programs FDR had started as part of the National Recovery Administration to fight the Depression.

"To the Editor," Uncle Hendrick began as soon as Kit was seated with pen and paper. "The NRA is a waste of taxpayers' money. It creates useless, make-work jobs so the government can hand out money to lazy idlers. FDR is drowning the USA in his alpha-bet soup of NRA programs, such as the CCC and the CWA."

Kit shifted in her chair. Uncle Hendrick knew perfectly well that last year Charlie had worked for the CCC, or Civilian Conservation Corps, in Montana for six months. Every month, Charlie had sent home twenty-five of the thirty dollars he earned. Her family had depended on it. Charlie liked his experience in the CCC so much that he hoped to sign up again. Uncle Hendrick also knew that the Civil Works Administration, or CWA, had given Dad the first job he'd had in almost two years. It was just a short-term, part-time, low-paying job clearing land and building stone walls out at the airport. But Dad was glad to be working again.

Kit loved seeing him go off to work, whistling and cheerful. He was proud of his work, and he thought it might lead to a better job that would use his skills as a mechanic. The other day at the hangar he'd met an old friend named Mr. Hesse who'd said that soon there might be work repairing airplane engines.

Kit pressed her lips together as Uncle Hendrick went on saying critical things about the very programs that were helping her family. "In short," Uncle Hendrick wound up, "when I say 'that man in the White House' is going to be the ruination of our fine country, all must agree."

I don't, thought Kit. But she kept her opinion to herself. She had learned that it was useless to argue with Uncle Hendrick. It was best to concentrate on keeping up with him and writing exactly what he said without misspelling any words. If the letter was not perfect, Uncle Hendrick pounced on the mistakes and ordered Kit to copy the whole thing over again. He was a stickler.

Kit handed him the letter. He read it, gave a curt nod of approval, then took the pen and signed it as well as he could with his hand in a cast. "They don't

print unsigned letters," he said. "Now, deliver this to
Mr. Gibson at the newspaper offices immediately. No
lollygagging!"

"Yes, sir," said Kit. Uncle Hendrick always acted as
if the newspaper editor was waiting breathlessly for his
letter and couldn't send the newspaper to press without
it. He was absolutely confident that his letter would
be printed. And rightly so, it seemed, because many of
his letters did appear in the newspaper. Kit thought it
was because he was rich and important. But she had to
admit that though she disagreed with what he said, she
admired how he said it. Uncle Hendrick expressed his
opinions forcefully. He never wasted a word. He said
precisely what he meant, with lots of vim and vigor.

Ruthie had left, and Stirling was busy drawing a
picture of Kit in her new coat for their newspaper. So
Kit went off on her errand alone. She knew the way
well: down the hill, past the beautiful fountain in the
center of the city, over two blocks and up one. The
newspaper offices were not far from the soup kitchen.
Kit saw lots of children in ragged coats and pitiful
shoes, but not the little girl to whom she had given her
coat. She hoped the girl and her mother were home, or

at least someplace safe and warm and comfortable.

Kit smiled as she went inside the big brick building that housed the newspaper offices. She climbed the stairs briskly, her footsteps *tsk-tsking* as she did. She could just imagine how Uncle Hendrick would *tsk-tsk* and sniff disdainfully if he knew how she loved to pretend that she was a reporter who worked in this building. She pushed open the door to the newsroom and was greeted with the clamor of telephones ringing, typewriters clacking, and people chatting. The noisy newsroom seemed like heaven to Kit. *This is where the newspaper is created,* she thought. *Stories that thousands of people will read are being written right here, right now.*

As she walked through the room to Mr. Gibson's desk, several people nodded to her. She'd delivered letters to the newspaper offices so many times that her face was familiar. Some of the friendlier reporters even knew her name. "Hi, Kit," one said as she passed by. "Got another letter for Gibb?"

"Yes, I do," Kit said. She knew they all called Mr. Gibson, the editor, "Gibb."

Gibb was not very friendly. He sat frowning behind his messy, cluttered desk. When Kit came near, he said without enthusiasm, "Put it in the box." He never even looked up.

"Yes, sir," said Kit. She put Uncle Hendrick's letter in Gibb's in-box on top of lots of other letters and a few rolls of film. Then she turned to go.

Kit wished she could linger in the newsroom. How she'd love to talk to the reporters! But she knew she had better hurry home to her chores. Saturday was the day she always washed all the sheets and put fresh ones on the boarders' beds. It also was the day she and Stirling went around the neighborhood selling eggs. After that, it would be time to help Mother with dinner. Kit was proud of the way she did her chores these days with great efficiency. *I bet I can find time to put the finishing touches on our newspaper,* she thought, *unless Uncle Hendrick has thought up something else for me to do.*

Letters with an "S"

n the last Sunday in February, Kit was trotting past the door to Uncle Hendrick's room with a laundry basket full of her clean clothes propped on her hip when she heard Uncle Hendrick call her.

"Kit, come here!" he barked. Inky barked, too, then followed up with a wheezy whine.

Kit stuck her head in the door. "Yes, sir?" she asked.

"Take a letter!" said Uncle Hendrick.

Not now! Kit thought. She'd been rushing to finish her chores ever since going out in the eerie early-morning light to get Uncle Hendrick's newspaper. Today was a special day. After lunch, Dad's friend Mr. Hesse was going to drive Dad and Kit and Charlie to the airport. Kit had already carefully put her camera in her coat pocket because she wanted to photograph Dad standing next to some of the stone walls he'd built. She also hoped Charlie would take *her* picture posed next to an airplane, just like her heroine, the pilot Amelia Earhart. Mother had said that Kit could use some of the egg money to have the film developed.

Reluctantly, Kit lowered the laundry basket, entered Uncle Hendrick's room, and picked up the pen and paper. She hoped the letter would be short.

"Start by writing, 'To the Editor,'" Uncle Hendrick instructed Kit, precisely as he had done many times before. Then he cleared his throat and dictated, "This morning I read on page twenty-five of your newspaper that an empty hospital in Covington, across the river from Cincinnati, may be used as a home for transients and unemployed persons."

Kit looked up. "Really?" she asked. "What a great idea!"

"Quiet!" growled Uncle Hendrick, echoed by Inky. Uncle Hendrick went on dictating, "This is an outrage! Such a home will attract tramps and drifters from all over the country. They'll flock here to be housed, fed, and clothed at our expense. We'll be pampering worth-less riffraff. All of these hoboes are men who have chosen to wander rather than work."

"Excuse me, Uncle Hendrick," Kit interrupted. She usually didn't say anything. But this time she had to speak up. "That's not true."

"I beg your pardon?" asked Uncle Hendrick icily.

"It's not true that all of the hoboes are men who have chosen to wander instead of working," Kit said. "Lots of them are on the road because they lost their jobs and their homes and they're trying to find work. And not all of the hoboes are men, either. Some are teenagers out on their own, some are women, and there are even whole families with little children."

Uncle Hendrick frowned at Kit. "Not another word out of you, Miss Impertinence," he said. "Write what I say. Keep your comments to yourself."

"Yes, sir," said Kit. She kept silent while Uncle Hendrick dictated the rest of his letter. But inside, she disagreed with every word.

"There!" said Uncle Hendrick, signing the letter. "Deliver this today."

Kit's heart sank as she took the letter. "But Uncle Hendrick," she protested. "I'm going to the airport with Dad and Charlie to take photos."

"No, you're not," said Uncle Hendrick, not the least bit sorry to be the bearer of bad news. "Mrs. Smithens came over earlier to tell your father that Mr. Hesse called. He doesn't want to drive anywhere because of the snow."

Kit looked out at the murky mid-morning sky. Snow was falling in a determined manner, as if it meant business. She sighed.

"Do as I say and deliver that letter," said Uncle Hendrick. "And do as I say and forget that nonsense you were blathering about earlier, too."

"It isn't nonsense," Kit insisted hotly, standing up to her uncle for once. "It's true. Hoboes are just poor people who are down on their luck."

"That," said Uncle Hendrick in a superior tone, "is just the kind of poppycock I'd expect your soft-headed parents to tell you."

It made Kit furious when Uncle Hendrick criticized her parents. "No one told me that," she said. "I learned it myself. I've been to the hobo jungle and to a soup kitchen, too."

"Whatever for?" asked Uncle Hendrick. He looked at Kit with unconcealed horror. "Hoboes are thieves and beggars. Why go near them?"

"I want to help," Kit said simply. "Especially the children."

"Ha!" scoffed Uncle Hendrick so loudly that Kit jumped and Inky yipped. "You're nothing but a child yourself, still caught up in babyish play, like making newspapers! What help could *you* be?" He raised his eyebrows. "I suppose you're planning to end the Depression single-handedly, is that it?"

"No, of course not," Kit said, hating how Uncle Hendrick made her feel so foolish, flushed, and flustered. "I don't mean that. I know I can't change much by myself. Not me alone." She tried to settle her rattled thoughts and speak sensibly. "I just think that if people knew about the hobo children, if they saw how terrible the children's coats and shoes are, I'm sure they'd help," she said. "And then the children would know that people cared about them, and that would give them hope, and—"

"Hope!" Uncle Hendrick cut in sharply. "An empty word. Comfort for fools. Hope never put a nickel in anybody's pocket, my girl, and hope is not going to end the Depression. Neither is pouring money into useless programs, or handing out coats or shoes to hobo children!" He dismissed Kit with a backward flutter of his hand, as if brushing away a tiresome fly. "Off with you," he said. "I, just like everyone else in the world, have better things to do than to listen to the jibber-jabber of a silly child like *you*. Go."

Kit left. She put Uncle Hendrick's letter in the laundry basket, wearily hoisted the basket onto her hip, then slowly trudged upstairs to her attic. Once there, she did not even have the energy to put her clothes away. Instead, she plunked down at her desk. Never had she felt so discouraged. Never had she felt such despair.

For almost two years, ever since Dad lost his job, she and her family had struggled through ups and downs, believing that if they worked hard enough, things would change for the better—not just for their family but for everyone hit hard by the Depression. It was that hope that kept them going. If Uncle Hendrick was right, if hope was for fools, what did they have left? The Depression had won, and there was nothing anyone could do. There was certainly nothing *she* could do to change anything. Uncle Hendrick had made that clear to her.

Tears welled in Kit's eyes. She put one elbow on either side of her typewriter and held her head in her hands. She sniffed hard, trying not to cry. Then she took a deep, shaky breath. Somehow, the dark, inky smell of the typewriter ribbon just under her nose comforted her, and so did the solid, clunky black bulk of the typewriter itself. Next to the typewriter, Kit saw the drawing Stirling had made for their newspaper. He'd drawn her striding along, her camera slung around her neck, wearing her new coat. *Chipper,* she said to herself. *That is the perfect word to describe how I look in Stirling's drawing. And what would be the perfect word to describe how I feel now? Crushed? Flattened? No. Squashed.* Idly, Kit touched the **s** key. She remembered how Dad had fixed it when the typewriter was broken. He had repaired the typewriter for her because he knew how much writing meant to her. Kit pushed down hard on the **s** and the key struck the paper with a satisfying *whack,* a sound that Kit loved.

Kit sat bolt upright. Suddenly, she knew what she must do: write!

If Uncle Hendrick could write letters to the newspaper, she could, too. She might not be rich or important, but she knew how to write a letter that said what she wanted it to say. She'd deliver her letter right along with Uncle Hendrick's. It might not appear in the newspaper, it might not change anything or anyone else, but writing it would change the way she felt.

Quickly, Kit rolled the paper with the **s** on it out of the typewriter so she could write her rough draft on the back of it. She picked up her pencil. *Now,* she thought, *how should I begin?* Then Kit grinned. "To the Editor," she wrote. Wasn't that what Uncle Hendrick had taught her? Hadn't he, in fact, taught her exactly how to write a letter to the newspaper? How many times had he said that a letter must have one point to make and must make it in simple, direct language, using not more than two hundred and fifty words? Hadn't he told her over and over again that letters must be signed or they wouldn't be printed? Without intending to, Uncle Hendrick had been a very helpful teacher because of all his hectoring and fusspot bossiness.

And Uncle Hendrick was not the only one helping Kit. As she wrote, she thought of Dad's dignity, Mother's industriousness, and the cheerful good nature of the boarders. She thought of Charlie, who'd come back from Montana with his "muscles grown hard, back grown strong, and heart grown stout," just as it said in the CCC booklet. She thought of steadfast Stirling, funny Ruthie, and how kind and neighborly Ruthie's family had been to hers. She thought about thrifty, ingenious Aunt Millie, who saved their house with her generosity; Will, the young hobo who had taught her about courage; and the little girl at the soup kitchen who'd brightened with hope when Kit gave her the old coat. Thinking about the way each one battled the Depression, its losses and fears, gave strength to what Kit wrote.

Kit worked on her letter for a long time. She chose her words carefully. She formed sentences in her head, then wrote and rewrote them till they sounded right. Then she read her rough draft aloud to herself:

To the Editor:

I think it is a good idea to use the hospital in Covington as a home to house, feed, and clothe hoboes. I have met some hoboes, and they are not all the same. Every hobo has his or her own story. Some hoboes chose a wandering life. Some people are hoboes because they lost their jobs and their homes and have nowhere to go. Some hoboes are grownups, some are young people, and there are even hobo families with little children. Though they all have different reasons for being on the road, I think all hoboes hope the road they're on will lead them to better times. But it is a long, hard trip, and they have nowhere to stay on the way. I think they deserve our help, sympathy, and compassion.

Hobo life is especially hard on children. They are often hungry and cold. Their coats and shoes are worn-out and outgrown. It would be a big help if people donated coats and shoes for children to soup kitchens and missions. It would show the children that we care about them, and that would give them hope. It would give all of us hope, too, because it would be a change for the better. Sometimes hope is all any of us, hoboes or not, have to go on.

Margaret Mildred Kittredge
Cincinnati, Ohio

Kit was pretty sure she had spelled *compassion* right. But something looked fishy about *sympathy*, and she didn't know whether *outgrown* was one word or two. Uncle Hendrick always said that there was no excuse for lazy spellers, and that a misspelled word made your reader lose confidence in you. So Kit looked up both *sympathy* and *outgrown* in the dictionary. When she was positive her spelling and punctuation were correct, she typed her letter very carefully. She struck every key hard, and with conviction. This time, Kit didn't care if the typewriter was noisy. Uncle Hendrick could hit the ceiling and Inky could howl and yowl. They were not going to stop her.

But there was no bluster or banging from below, and Kit was able to finish her letter in peace. She was folding it to put it into an envelope when Ruthie and Stirling came up the attic stairs.

"Hey, Kit," said Ruthie. "Want to come with Stirling and me? I've got some shoes and coats that're too small for me, and we're bringing them to the soup kitchen."

"Sure," said Kit. "Then after, I have some letters to deliver to the newspaper office."

"Letters with an 's'?" asked Stirling. "You mean Uncle Hendrick dictated two today?"

Kit smiled. "No," she said. "One is mine."

The Perfect Word

 s they walked to the soup kitchen, Kit told Ruthie and Stirling about her argument with Uncle Hendrick and her decision to write a letter of her own. "I had to," she said. "Not just because I think he's wrong about the hoboes, but also because I felt so terrible when he said that hope was for fools."

"Well!" said Ruthie indignantly, her cheeks bright and her eyes snappy. "If you ask me, I think Uncle Hendrick is foolish *and* hopeless."

Snow was falling thick and fast. Enough had accumulated on the ground that the children kicked up cascades of it as they walked.

"Let's hurry," said Stirling. "It's getting slippery."

"I bet they'll have to call off school tomorrow," said Ruthie joyfully.

"Hurray!" cheered Kit and Stirling. "No school!" After that, the children didn't talk much. It was too hard to talk, because the wind was blowing the snow into their faces. Kit pulled her hat down over her ears and held her collar closed over her mouth. She bent forward, her shoulders hunched. The wind seemed to be coming from every direction at once. Sometimes it pushed against Kit as if trying to stop her. Then suddenly it would swoop around and push her from behind as if it were trying to hasten her along.

Kit thought it was a very good thing that she and Ruthie and Stirling knew the way to River Street so well. They had to walk with their eyes squinted shut against the stinging snow. Slowly they made their way to the alley behind the soup kitchen and up to its back door. They stopped to stomp the snow off their boots before they opened the door and went inside. The cooking area was busier than ever. And when the three children pushed through the big swinging door, they saw that the front room where the food was served was terribly crowded because of the harsh, wet weather.

"Oh, my," whispered Kit in dismay. The room

smelled of wet wool. It seemed to Kit to be awash in a
sea of gray, filled as it was with people wearing their
snow-soaked winter coats and hats.

"I think," said Ruthie firmly, "we should give my
old coats and shoes to someone in charge. I don't see
how we'd choose who needs them most."

Kit agreed. The hobo children's coats and shoes
were even worse than she remembered. They were so
worn-out and filthy! They were such pitiful protection
against the cold and wet of a day like today.

Stirling asked a woman serving food, and she
pointed out the director of the soup kitchen. It took the
three children a while to wriggle their way through the
crowd to her. The room was so packed, it was hard not
to jostle anyone or step on anyone's feet.

When they finally reached the director, Ruthie said,
"Excuse me, ma'am. We brought these coats and shoes.
We were hoping you'd give them to some children who
need them."

"Why, thank you," said the director as she took the
things from Ruthie. "I'll have no trouble finding new
owners for these." She sighed. "Not many people think
of the children. We have more and more children

passing through here now, and all are in such
desperate need."

After the director spoke, Kit remembered her own
voice saying to Uncle Hendrick, *"If people knew about
the hobo children . . ."* Kit slid her hand into her pocket
to be sure her letter to the newspaper about the hobo
children was safe. As she did, she felt something hard
in her pocket. It was her camera. Again, she heard her
own voice. This time it was saying, *"If they saw how
terrible the children's coats and shoes are, I'm sure they'd
help."*

Kit had an idea. Eagerly, she took her camera out
of her pocket. "Would it be all right if we took some
photographs of the children?" she asked the director.

"You must ask the children's permission and their
parents', too," answered the director. "If they say yes,
it's all right with me."

"Thanks!" said Kit. She and Ruthie and Stirling
shared a quick grin. Kit did not even have to explain
her brainstorm to her friends. They figured it out right
away.

"We'll put the film in the envelope with your letter,"
said Ruthie.

"As I always say, a picture tells more about a person than words ever could," said Stirling.

Then they went into action. It was quite remarkable, Kit thought, how well they worked as a team. Without even talking about it, each one took a separate job. Ruthie asked the children if they'd like to have their pictures taken and explained politely to the parents what Kit wanted to do. Stirling told the children where to sit or stand and arranged their coats so that they'd show up clearly in the picture.

Kit worked the camera. She didn't have a flash, so she had to use light from the window. First she took pictures that showed the children from head to toe. Then she took pictures of the children's feet and makeshift shoes. Some children had taken their shoes off and lined them up to dry by a hissing radiator. Kit took a picture of the sad parade of shoes, which looked as exhausted as the children to whom they belonged. None of the shoes looked as if they could go another step.

Too soon, Kit had used all her film. "That's it," she said to Ruthie and Stirling. She put the film in the envelope with her letter. "Let's go."

The snowstorm was cruel and furious now. As Kit led Ruthie and Stirling to the newspaper offices, the children were blown and buffeted by the ice-cold wind. Every inch of the way was hard-won. It was a great relief to go inside the big brick building and be out of the swirling snow. It was very warm inside. Snow melted off the children's coats and boots and left a wet trail behind them as they climbed the stairs and walked through the newsroom to Gibb's desk.

Kit took the two letters out of her pocket, then hesitated. *Plip, plop.* The snow melting off her coat made an apologetic sound as it dripped to the floor. A small puddle formed around Kit's feet. Drops from her hat hit the letters.

"Put it in the box," ordered Gibb with even more impatience and less enthusiasm than usual. As always, he did not bother to look up.

Kit took a deep breath. She put the letter from Uncle Hendrick in the in-box. Under it she slid her own letter, which was bulgy with the roll of film and rather damp and wrinkled.

The three children left the newsroom and walked down the stairs. "Do you suppose they'll use the photos we took?" asked Stirling as the children paused to prepare themselves to face the storm before they went out of the newspaper office building.

"I don't know," Kit said.

"I wonder if they'll print your letter," mused Ruthie as she pulled on her mittens. "And if they do print it, do you think it'll change anything?"

"I don't know that, either," said Kit. She grinned crookedly. "Don't tell Uncle Hendrick, but I *hope* so."

❇

The world was quiet, clean, and innocent under its fresh white layer of snow the next morning when Kit went out to walk Inky and buy Uncle Hendrick's newspaper. Uncle Hendrick always pitched a fit if his newspaper had been unfolded and read before he got it. So, even though she was bursting with curiosity, Kit knew she must not open up the paper to see if her letter and the photos had been printed. She had pretty much convinced herself that Gibb had tossed them in the trash. Still, it was hard not to feel optimistic on a beautiful morning like this, with the sun making a sparkling prism of every flake that caught its reflection.

Kit delivered the newspaper, his breakfast tray, and Inky to Uncle Hendrick. She fiddled awhile undoing the leash from Inky's collar, hoping that Uncle Hendrick would open up the newspaper and turn to the editorial page. But instead, Uncle Hendrick turned to her and said, "I don't want you now." So Kit had to leave.

She went downstairs and helped Mother serve breakfast to the boarders. They were all seated at the table when suddenly they heard Uncle Hendrick bellow and Inky yowl. Kit jumped up to go see what was the matter. But before she took a step, Uncle Hendrick exploded out of his room and came clomping down the stairs, with Inky yip-yapping close behind him. "What's the meaning of this?" Uncle Hendrick shouted, waving the newspaper over his head.

Kit sat down hard. *Could it be?* she wondered.

"Hello, Uncle Hendrick," said Mother, trying to calm him. "We are so pleased to see you back on your feet again!"

"Never mind," growled Uncle Hendrick. He slapped the newspaper onto the table, setting all the china rattling and making the silverware clink.

Ignoring everyone else, he glared at Kit. "What have you done, young lady?"

Kit kicked Stirling under the table. They both tried to hide their smiles.

"I might have known you were in on it, too," Uncle Hendrick said to Stirling. "Young whippersnapper!"

"What is going on?" asked Dad. He picked up the newspaper and exclaimed, "Well, for heaven's sakes! There's a letter to the editor here from Kit. And there are photos with it, too!"

Pandemonium broke loose. Everyone jumped up from the table, all talking at once, and crowded around Dad to get a look at the newspaper. They didn't pay any attention to Uncle Hendrick, who was standing in the background making an angry speech to no one, pounding the floor with his cane, his remarks punctuated by Inky's barks. Grace, who loved mayhem, added her hoarse woofs to the hubbub, too.

"Settle down!" Dad called out. When everyone was quiet, even Uncle Hendrick and Inky, Dad said, "I'm going to read Kit's letter aloud. I want everyone to listen."

Kit felt a warm blush begin at her toes and climb all

the way up to the top of her head as Dad read her letter. Mother came and stood behind Kit's chair and put her hands on Kit's shoulders. When Dad had finished reading, she said, "Kit, I'm proud of you!" She leaned down and kissed Kit's cheek.

This was too much for Uncle Hendrick. "Proud?" he said, aghast. "Proud of that impudent girl?" He pointed an angry finger at Kit. "And you, a mere child, writing a letter to the newspaper! Where did you get such an idea?"

"Why, from you, of course, Uncle Hendrick," answered Kit politely.

Uncle Hendrick was speechless. A strange expression crossed his face. It seemed to be a mixture of annoyance and something that could have been respect. It lasted only a moment. Then Uncle Hendrick turned away and stalked off, Inky trailing behind him.

After that, everyone congratulated Kit, and Stirling, too. But Kit barely heard them. She held the newspaper in her two hands and looked at her letter and the photographs. Thousands of people would read this newspaper and see the photos. Thousands of people would read words that *she* had written. Kit shivered with delight. She could hardly believe it was true.

❈

Ruthie was right. School *was* closed that day because of the snow. In fact, school was closed for a week after the storm, which turned out to have been the worst blizzard to hit Cincinnati in years.

So it was more than a week later, at the end of the first day back, that Kit, Ruthie, and Stirling found themselves walking to the soup kitchen after school. Lots of Kit's classmates had read her letter and seen the photos in the newspaper. They had brought their old coats and shoes to school. Some of Kit and Stirling's egg customers had also seen the letter and the photos, and they had made donations of clothing, too. Kit and Stirling were staggering under armloads of coats, and Ruthie was pulling the wagon, which was full of boots and shoes. They brought their donations straight to the director of the soup kitchen.

The director smiled broadly at them. "I am so glad to see the three of you!" she said. "You're the children who took the photos, aren't you?"

Kit, Ruthie, and Stirling nodded.

The director asked Kit, "And are you the one who wrote the letter?"

"Yes, ma'am," said Kit.

"We've had many more donations for the children since your letter and those photos appeared in the newspaper," said the director. "You drew attention to a real need. You three have truly made a difference. Thank you."

"You're welcome," said Kit, Ruthie, and Stirling, beaming.

As it happened, Kit had another letter of Uncle Hendrick's to deliver to the newspaper office. This one was about Eleanor Roosevelt. Uncle Hendrick highly disapproved of the work she was doing to help miners in West Virginia. The letter was so full of fiery words that Kit was surprised it wasn't hot to the touch.

This time, it was a quick, easy walk to the newspaper building, since the weather was clear. Upstairs, the newsroom was just as noisy and busy as ever, and Gibb was as distracted as always when the children came to his desk. Kit started to put Uncle Hendrick's letter in Gibb's in-box.

"Hold on," said Gibb. Kit stopped.

Gibb tilted his head toward the letter. "Is that one of his or one of yours?" he asked.

"His," Kit answered.

"Put it in the box," said Gibb in his usual brusque way. Then his voice changed. "But any time you've got something else *you* want to write, bring it here. You've got the makings of a good reporter, kid."

Kit was so happy she could hardly speak. "Thanks," she said. Out of the corner of her eye, she saw Ruthie and Stirling nudge each other and grin.

The three of them walked home together along the slushy sidewalks, dodging puddles of melted snow. But the sky was blue overhead, and there was a certain softness in the air that seemed to Kit to carry the scent of spring. It was just a hint, just a whiff, but it was full of promise.

That's it, thought Kit. *That's the perfect word. I feel full of **promise.***

INSIDE Kit's World

During the Depression—long before the word *recycle* was ever used—people saved or recycled everything. Their motto was, "Use it up, wear it out, make it do, or do without." Mothers cut up their old clothes to make clothing for their children. They turned coats inside out and resewed them to make them look new, as Mother did for Kit. They turned worn-out clothes into quilts, braided rugs, or cleaning rags. Even the cloth sacks that animal feed came in, which were printed in colorful patterns, became aprons, pajamas, doll clothes, or dresses like the one Aunt Millie made for Kit.

Like the Kittredges, families also found ways to have fun with little money. They spent more time at home together reading library books, listening to the radio, doing jigsaw puzzles, and playing card games. Parties with homemade food and decorations, like Kit's Penny-Pincher Party, were just as much fun as ones with store-bought food and decor.

Families who lost their homes had harder times. Some packed all their belongings into their cars and went in search of new jobs. Others, like Kit's friend Will, hopped onto freight trains and rode the rails, with only a bedroll and the clothes they wore. Hopping freights was illegal and dangerous, but hoboes couldn't afford to travel any other way. When a train pulled into a new town, the hoboes got off and started looking for work.

Some knocked on doors to ask for food in exchange for doing chores. Like Will, most hoboes brought food back to the *jungles*, the hobo camps near rail yards. There, they added it to the large pots of stew to share with others. Even though hoboes helped one another and often found a special sort of community in the jungles, hobo life was harsh and difficult.

When he was running for president, Franklin Delano Roosevelt promised a "New Deal" to put people back to work. One of his first programs was the Civilian Conservation Corps, or CCC, which put thousands of young men to work building and improving parks, planting trees, and fighting fires. CCC workers were sent to outdoor work camps all over the country, where they earned $30 per month, $25 of which they had to send home to their families. The next time you go to a state or national park, look for a CCC marker on signs and buildings!

Another New Deal program—still in effect today—was the Social Security Administration, which provided and protected retirement funds for American workers and a safety net for those unable to work. Many Americans were grateful for these programs, but others, like Kit's Uncle Hendrick, did not like what they thought of as government "meddling" in business and citizens' lives. People with strong opinions about the New Deal and the Depression argued their viewpoints in the newspaper, just like Kit and Uncle Hendrick!

Read more of KIT'S stories,

available from booksellers and at *americangirl.com*

❧ *Classics* ❧

Kit's classic series, now in two volumes:

Volume 1:
Read All About It!
Kit has a nose for news.
When the Great Depression
hits home, Kit's newsletters
begin making a real impact.

Volume 2:
Turning Things Around
With Dad still out of work,
Kit wonders if things will ever
get better. Could a letter to the
newspaper make a difference?

❧ *Journey in Time* ❧

Travel back in time—and spend a day with Kit!

Full Speed Ahead

Help Kit outwit Uncle Hendrick, find a missing puppy, and stay
out of jail when she's caught riding a freight train like a hobo! You
get to choose your own path through this multiple-ending story.

❧ *Mysteries* ❧

More thrilling adventures with Kit!

Intruders at Rivermead Manor
What's really going on in the old mansion next door?

Missing Grace
Kit's beloved basset hound has disappeared without a trace.

A Thief in the Theater
Can Kit catch the thief before the theater closes its doors for good?

Danger at the Zoo
With her reporter's instinct, Kit sniffs out some monkey business!

❋ *A Sneak Peek at* ❋

Full Speed Ahead

My Journey with Kit

Meet Kit and take an unforgettable journey
in a book that lets *you* decide what happens.

eep, bee-dle-lee beep beep, beep beep. It's my phone. My best friend Isabel has just sent me a photo of her pet bunny, Pippa. She is *so cute!*

I call Isabel. "Pippa is adorable," I say. "You are so lucky, Izza! I've asked my mom a million times to let me have a pet."

"And?" Isabel asks.

I sigh, "Sometimes she jokes that my room is so messy a pet would get lost in it. And sometimes she's serious and says that having a pet is a big deal and I'm not responsible enough."

Isabel says, "You were responsible about going to that science day camp thingy this summer—"

"Camp Mosquito!" That's what I called it, anyway. I still have a constellation of bites on my leg in the shape of the Big Dipper.

"You went every day even though you don't especially like creepy-crawlies like bugs or worms."

"Or *sssnakessss*," I hiss.

Isabel giggles. "And I bet you've been responsible about writing that essay for the first day of school tomorrow, right?"

Uh-oh.

"The *what*?" I gulp. "For *when*?"

"The essay," says Isabel, "due tomorrow."

Terrific. Fifth grade starts tomorrow, and I'm already behind.

Isabel goes on. "You're supposed to write a paragraph about the most important idea you learned this summer."

"Seriously? That's the most boring topic in the world! What did you write about?"

"Pippa," says Isabel, "and how pets teach us about love. Hey! I know what—you could write about Camp Mosquito."

"Mmm-hmm," I say. "How's this?" I put on a deep voice and pretend I'm reading aloud. "The most important idea I learned at science camp is that bug spray isn't repellent but Harry Sharma is. The end."

Isabel giggles mischievously. "You know Harry only teases you to get your attention, because he has a crush on you."

"Ee-ew!" I protest. "News flash: Harry Sharma is obnoxious and stuck-up and annoying," I tell her, leaving no room for argument. "Listen, Izza, I'd better go. If I start now and write all night long, I *might* get a paragraph written by dawn."

"Okay," Isabel says. "Call me later?"

"Of course," I say. "Bye."

❋

I wander into the kitchen to make a snack, thinking about Isabel and how she and her big noisy family are crammed into a teeny house, while I'm an only child rattling around in this humongous super-sleek apartment with my mom—when my mom is here, which she usually isn't. Most of the time, like right now, she's at work. So it's just Sophie the babysitter and me.

I wave to Sophie as I walk through the living room. She gives me a brief smile but keeps on texting, ignoring me as usual. I think: *If I had a dog, I wouldn't feel so lonely.* Before I turn on the kitchen light, I look out the window. Mom and I live on the top floor of our high-rise, and the walls of our apartment are glass. It's not what you'd call cozy, but I like our apartment at times like right now, when I have a bird's-eye view of the city spread out below me, and lights are twinkling from every building around me. It's as if there's a soft, starry night sky above me *and* below me, and the starry skies meet at the horizon. It gives me a restless, shivery feeling.

I open the refrigerator and see a microwave-safe dish wrapped in plastic with a note from Mom on it:

> Heat for 5 minutes.
> Early bed. School tomorrow!
> Love and kisses, Mom ☺

Haiku, if you don't count the smiley face. I sort of forgot about dinner, and now it's too late to eat it, so I just grab an apple and go back to my room.

My desk is too messy to sit at because I left my grungy softball glove and tennis racket and balls and socks and towels and about a hundred books on it. (I love to read.) I take my laptop and sit on the floor. I type:

The Most Important Idea I Learned This Summer

I stare at that, but I can't think of anything to write except *I wish I had a dog.*

Mom always turns the air-conditioning to sub-zero, so my room is as cold as an iceberg. I grab an old coat out of my project suitcase and snuggle into it. My project suitcase is full of old clothes I'm planning to work on. That's my hobby: going to thrift stores and buying old, vintage clothes. Some of the clothes—like the coat, which I think is from the 1950s—are so cool that I wear them as is. Others I cut apart and reassemble in a totally new way for myself. I know it's a useless kind of hobby, just sort of silly and frivolous. But I don't inflict my creations on anyone, and Mom doesn't seem to mind. She says I'm fearless with the scissors.

In my project suitcase I also find an odd, heavy, rectangular sort of box. It's a camera—a *really* old-fashioned one. It's funky, but cool, with a leather strap. It must have come with a box of clothes; I don't remember buying it. Carefully, I open it up and look down at it into the viewing slot, as if I'm taking a photo. I wonder if it works—does it even have film in it? Slowly, I press the shutter button . . . *click.*

And then,

and then,

and then . . .

I realize it sounds weird and impossible, but the next thing I know, it's broad daylight, I'm in the leafy front yard of a big house, camera still in hand, and a girl who's about my age is walking toward me. And just as weird, right next to me there's a wiggly golden retriever puppy, acting as though he belongs to me and is my best buddy. I pick him up and hold him. If this is a dream, it's a dream come true about the puppy.

"Hi," says the girl, smiling politely.

"Hi," I croak.

"I'm Kit Kittredge," says the girl. "We've been expecting you. You must be Cousin Lucille."

"Lucille?" I repeat. "No." I want to say that I'm not Kit's cousin, and that Lucille is not my name, but I just stammer, "Lu . . . Lu—"

"Oh, okay, I'll call you Lulu if you want," Kit says.

Lulu? Why not? When something's so extreme that it's crazy, don't you call it a lulu? This experience I'm having right now is definitely a lulu.

Kit reaches out and scratches the puppy behind the ears. "Hi there," Kit says to him. She smiles at me, and this time her smile is big and genuine, not stiff and polite like before. "What's your dog's name?"

"He isn't my dog," I tell her. "I don't know who he belongs to."

The puppy licks me on the chin. "He sure seems

to think that he belongs to you," Kit says with a grin. "He has no collar or tags. So unless someone claims him, it looks like he's yours if you want him."

"Oh, I do!" I exclaim. "I want a dog more than anything!"

Kit nods. It's clear that she understands completely. "So what are you going to call him?" she asks.

"Buddy," I say. It's the name I've always imagined for my dog, ever since I was little, because that's what I want a dog for—to be my buddy.

"Buddy," says Kit. "That's a cute name. I have a dog named Grace. I love her like crazy. Come on inside and meet her. Everyone will be glad that you're here."

❉ *To go in and meet Grace,*
   turn to page 20.

❉ *To tell Kit I'm not Cousin Lucille,*
   turn to page 11.

About the Author

VALERIE TRIPP says that she became
a writer because of the kind of person she is.
She says she's curious, and writing requires
you to be interested in everything. Talking
is her favorite sport, and writing is a way of
talking on paper. She's a daydreamer, which
helps her come up with her ideas. And she
loves words. She even loves the struggle
to come up with just the right words as
she writes and rewrites. Ms. Tripp lives in
Maryland with her husband.